Lesson Learned

Earl Sewell

Lesson Learned

LESSON LEARNED

ISBN-13: 978-0-373-83116-6
ISBN-10: 0-373-83116-1

www.KimaniTRU.com

Printed in U.S.A.

Acknowledgments

In late 2007, Hillcrest and Homewood Flossmoor High Schools invited me to come speak to their students about *Keysha's Drama,* which is the first book in this series. At the time I learned that *Keysha's Drama* was very popular among the students at both schools. In March of 2008, I spoke at Hillcrest High. Initially I thought I'd be speaking to about twenty students. However to my delight and surprise around fifty students signed up and attended my presentation. Most of them had read *Keysha's Drama,* and the others were in the process of reading it. As I stood before them explaining my background and the joys of my career as an author, I got the sense that students were eager to start the book discussion. The moment I transitioned and began to talk about Keysha and her drama, it was on. We talked about my character as if she were a real person and would be walking through the door at any moment. The school's principal, librarian and other faculty in attendance were all very excited to see their students talking so passionately about a book. I made their energy my own and in return received something extraordinary. So I say thank you to all of the students at Hillcrest High School who read the book and participated in my discussion. I'd also like to send out a very special thank-you to Ms. Lisa Walsh and Ms. Andrea Collins, who worked very hard to arrange my visit. Thank you to Mrs. Renee Simms, the principal at Hillcrest who helped fund the event. An additional thank-you goes out to Dr. Marcia Mendenhall (Assistant Superintendent of Instruction) and Ms. Heidi Horne (Dr. Mendenhall's assistant), who ordered and provided the funds for copies of *Keysha's Drama.*

A few weeks later, I was at Homewood Flossmoor High School, standing in a lecture hall speaking to well over one hundred students! Many of them had read the book, and others were interested in becoming published authors. I met one young lady who'd already written a book! I was so impressed with her and encouraged her to keep writing. So to all of the students at Homewood Flossmoor High School, I say thank you. I would also like to thank Ms. Jane Harper and her staff for working so diligently on my behalf.

In June of 2008, I went to visit the students at the Marine Military Academy. These students stayed after school to meet with me and talk about *Keysha's Drama,* the process of writing and how to bring fiction to life. We had a blast during the improvisation segment of my workshop. The Marine Military Academy has several future actors and actresses on the horizon. I want to thank all of the students who attended and especially

Ms. Diana Wendt, who set up the event. Another thank-you to the school principal, Mr. Paul Stroh, Assistant Principal Kim Hinton and the school clerk, Ms. Cansella Hale, who provided refreshments and the books for the event.

I have so many people to thank for my continuing success in this profession. I have to give a big thank-you to my editor Glenda Howard, who has stood with me and helped give birth to this wonderful series. To Ladoris Hope and Lindell Slaughter, who are two of my biggest fans. Ya'll know that I have mad love for you. Thank you to all the book clubs around the country who've been supporting and encouraging me for years. Another thank-you goes out to all of you who have e-mailed me or contacted me through MySpace and Facebook. I truly appreciate your kind words and your love of the series. To Ms. Farelle Walker, my cover model who is also an actress on BET's *Hell Date.* Thank you so much for doing a wonderful job capturing the essence of my character Keysha. You're such a gifted woman and I wish you much success in your career.

In case I forgot anyone, which I often do, please forgive me and know that I am truly grateful for all your assistance.

Please feel free to drop me a line at earl@earlsewell.com. Please put the title of my book in the subject line so that I know your message to me is not spam. Make sure you check out www.earlsewell.com and www.myspace.com/earlsewell. Also visit the fictional character Keysha at www.myspace.com/keyshasdrama.

All my best,

Earl Sewell

Today I celebrate the death of the word “can’t.”
—Alicia Keys

one

KEYSHA
Friday, November 2nd

"wesley, I'm still freaking out!" I said as I took a sip of my pink lemonade. It was Friday afternoon and we were sitting inside a Mr. Submarine restaurant eating lunch. Wesley wearing blue jeans with a black turtleneck looked scrumptious. I, on the other hand, looked like a bum. I had on an oversize gray jogging outfit and a black baseball cap to hide my messy hair, and the breakage around my hairline. The sudden loss of my hair was a sign of how stressed out I'd been over the past week. Just after I'd cleared up all of the mess that occured two months ago with my enemy Liz Lloyd, who planted drugs on me and the court case that could've put me behind bars, my mother, Justine, recently released from jail, decided to resurface. She was hell-bent on ruining my life by demanding that I pack my bags and move back to the hood with her. Wesley, the best boyfriend a girl could ever wish for, listened to my every word as I told him about the drama I went through with my deranged mother.

"Keysha, I can't believe that your mother actually showed up at your dad's house last weekend and demanded that you come live with her," Wesley said as he took a bite of his sandwich. "That's jacked up," he said trying to chew his food and talk at the same time. "How could she actually think that you wanted to go back and live with her after all she's done?"

"I don't know, but moving back into the house with her is the last thing that I want to do. I'd rather go to jail and be cell mates with Liz Lloyd before going back to live under the same roof with her," I said as I glanced out of the window noticing a cluster of Thornwood students bundling up to fight off the bitterly cold air as they moved hurriedly down South Park Boulevard. It wouldn't be long before we'd have to deal with subzero temperatures and heavy, wet snow. I turned my attention back to Wesley.

"I was so horrified when I opened the door and saw my mother's face. I literally froze up. I was completely speechless and you know it takes a lot for me to be at a loss for words. Then, before I could even process that it was really her, she started yelling at me and demanding that I pack my bags and leave with her and her ugly ex-convict boyfriend. That entire scene was just too much for my mind to process so I fainted right there at the door." I paused to brush away with my napkin the mustard that was at the corner of Wesley's mouth.

"Do I have anything else on me?" Wesley asked as he picked up a napkin and dabbed the other side of his mouth.

"No, you're good. Just stop chewing your food so fast," I said as I released a depressing sigh.

"Now, run it by me once again. How did she find you?" Wesley asked as he swirled a french fry in a small cup of ketchup.

"Her boyfriend, Simon, is my dad's cousin. I suppose I owe the guy a little bit of gratitude because he was one of the people who helped me find my father."

"How did he help you find your dad?" Wesley asked, confused.

"It's a long story, boo. But the short and sweet story is that Simon introduced my dad, Jordan, to my mother when they were younger. My dad had a weird one-night encounter with my mother and produced me. My father never saw my mother again after that and pretty much didn't even know I existed. A lot of time passed, both my mom and Simon were on and off of drugs as well as in and out of jail. Then one day, Simon reentered my mom's life and I guess they started dating or something. Anyway, when Simon got a chance to see me again, he helped my mother make the connection as to who my father was. Blah, blah, blah and the rest is history. Keysha Kendall: A tragic life." I forced myself to laugh a little.

"Your dad must have been mad as hell when your mother showed up unannounced with his cousin." Wesley took a sip of his drink.

"Oh, Jordan blew his top and it wasn't a pretty sight. When he came to the door and saw me sprawled out on the floor, he thought that Simon and my mother had done something to me. He started yelling, "What did you do to her?" over and over again. All of Jordan's yelling snapped me out of my foggy state of mind. Jordan then helped me to my feet and escorted me back inside and over to the sofa. By that time, Barbara had gotten out of bed to see what all of the ruckus was about. Jordan had gone back to the door to deal with Simon and Justine.

"Is she okay?" I heard Simon ask. "Why did she fall out like that?"

"Simon, what are you doing here?" I heard my dad ask. I could hear intense anger in his voice.

"Is that any way to greet your long lost cousin, man?" Simon snapped back at him.

"Damn, you look good," I heard my mother say.

"Who is that at the door?" Barbara, my stepmother, asked as she exited from the nearby bathroom with a cold towel to place on my forehead.

"You don't want to know," I answered as she pressed the towel against my skin. I closed my eyes for a moment and tried to make sense of everything that was happening.

"I came by so that Justine could see the daughter you two share. You remember Justine, don't you? I know it's been a few years." It was no secret that my dad didn't like him. They had some kind of rivalry that dated back to their childhood.

"I vaguely remember her," Jordan said. I could tell that he was not feeling the fact that his past had shown up at his doorstep unannounced and unexpected.

"I just want to see my daughter and make sure she's okay," Justine said as if she were really concerned.

"You should have been thinking about her well-being when you abandoned her." Barbara moved toward the doorway. I could tell that she was supremely ticked off as well once she realized who was at her door. I was in a funny place at that moment, confused. I didn't like the fact that my mother had shown up but I also didn't want Jordan and Barbara snapping on her. Don't ask me why I felt that way. I just did.

"And who are you?" Justine's quick and ugly temper reared its repulsive head.

"I'm the woman who is about to slam the door in your face," Barbara said as she planted herself next to Jordan.

"Now hold on a minute, Barbara. Justine and I are like family. I know it would have been more proper to call and set something up, but Justine wanted to surprise Keysha. I wasn't thinking when I drove her over here. I made a mistake. I'm human, what can I say?" Simon tried to sound as if his unwanted visit was no big deal.

"Stop lying!" I finally stood up and moved toward the door. "You guys came here to take me away. Justine said it herself. She told me to pack my things."

"Is that true, Simon? You were coming here to take Keysha away?" Jordan asked.

"Hey," Simon shrugged his shoulders and exposed the

palms of his hands. "I don't know anything about that. I was just doing a favor for my old friend Justine."

"Oh, now I'm just an old friend?" Justine snapped at Simon.

"Simon, I can see right through your bull," Jordan said. "Don't ever come to my house again unannounced and uninvited. Now leave, before I call the police and have you escorted off my property." Jordan slammed the door shut.

I heard my mother's muffled voice through the closed door. From what I could tell, she was upset with Simon for referring to her as an old friend.

"Damn, that's messed up," said Wesley as he leaned back in his chair. "What do you think is going to happen?"

"What do you mean?" I asked confused.

"Well, how do you feel about your mother wanting you to come back and live with her?"

"I'm *not* going back to live with her. She's crazy if she thinks that I am," I said as I scratched my forearm, which immediately turned red. "What the hell—" I paused as I looked at my skin, wondering why I suddenly broke out with hives. "Look at this," I thrust my arm at Wesley.

"Dang, what do you have?" he asked, wrinkling his brow.

"What do you mean, what do I have? It flared up just now," I said as I continued to scratch. Wesley was silent and didn't say anything. I could tell that he didn't want to touch me and risk contracting hives.

"It's nothing. I'll be okay. I'll just put some hydrocortisone cream on it," I said trying to assure him.

"Are you sure? I'm worried about you, Keysha," Wesley admitted.

"For once in my life, I'd just like things to be normal, you know," I said wistfully as I willed myself to stop scratching.

"Why do you think your mom wants you back?" Wesley asked.

"I have no clue. But knowing my mother the way that I do, she doesn't want me back because she misses me. There is a reason." I laughed a little. "There's always a reason when it comes to my mom."

"I know what you mean. My mom hasn't missed a beat either. Can you believe that she's still trying to get access to my dad's checking account? Just because she knows that I'm taking care of his affairs while he's recovering, she thinks she can strong-arm me into robbing my own father."

"Why doesn't she just give up? I mean, can't she see that you're not going to cave in to her?" I asked. At that moment my other arm began to itch. I resisted temptation to scratch.

"Please. My mother is going to keep on trying until she gets what she wants." Wesley said.

"How is your dad doing?" I asked.

"Better." Wesley paused. "Keysha, there is something I need to tell you—"

"Ooh," I cut Wesley off and began scratching my other

arm vigorously. I coiled back the sleeve on my sweater and saw that my other arm was covered with red hives.

"Come on. Let me walk you back home, Keysha. That rash doesn't look pretty and you're beginning to make me itch," he said as he started scratching the side of his neck.

"I'm not diseased, Wesley," I said because I could tell that my sudden outbreak had grossed him out.

"I know, but obviously something isn't right."

"Fine." I said as I repositioned my cap and reached for my coat. Wesley picked up our trays and tossed our wrappers and empty soda cups in the garbage. As we stepped out into the chilly November air, my body began to shiver.

"Dang. I'm going to have to go in the house, turn on the oven and stand in front of it to get warm," I said as we walked faster. "Are the construction workers done with your house yet? Do you have heat in there?"

"No. They're not done yet. They've run into some problems and it's going to take longer than they anticipated."

"What's the problem?" I asked.

"The fire melted a lot of the mechanicals and ventilation ducts in the house. They have to redo the heating and cooling vents in the house, replace the plumbing as well as the water heater, furnace and a lot of other stuff."

"You can't stay in a house with no heat. You'll freeze to death. Chicago in the winter time is no joke. The wind chill can make it feel as if it's twenty degrees below zero." I was really concerned for Wesley. His house had caught on fire a few weeks ago after his father attempted to install a ceiling fan. Wesley's dad was injured pretty seriously and he was still recovering from his injuries.

"I know how bad the winter months can be. But I'm not going to freeze to death, I promise you that."

"Then how are you going to make it through the winter in a house that doesn't have heat?" I asked.

Wesley paused and looked at the ground. I immediately sensed that something was wrong.

"Wesley? What's going on? Is your dad okay? He's going to pull through, right?" I'd gotten nervous because I thought something terrible had happened to his dad who was still in the hospital.

"It's—" I held up my hand to interrupt him. "Don't tell me that Liz or her drug dealer boyfriend, Neophus, have threatened you or did something to your dad." I was running through a list of possible issues that Wesley might have.

"No. It's not that. I'm not worried about backlash from Liz or Neophus. I'm just glad all of that is over and we don't have to deal with them anymore."

"Then, what is it?" I asked.

"Keysha. My dad is getting out soon and we won't be able to live in our house this winter. My dad and I are moving—to another state."

I stopped walking and glared at him. At first, I thought he was just joking, but the sad look in his eyes told me that he wasn't. I felt as if my heart had stopped and I suddenly found it difficult to breathe.

two

MIKE
Saturday, November 3rd

Thornwood students had traveled all the way across town to our opponent's school to support our team. There was only one minute and thirty seconds left in the championship football game against the Titans. They were the most formidable opponents my team has ever had to battle. Today the Titans were thumping so hard that they'd sent Romeo, our punt returner, on an ambulance ride to the hospital with a broken arm. The Titans had a quarterback with a golden arm, a running back who was powerful and difficult to tackle and two lighting-fast, track-and-field champions as wide receivers.

It didn't look good for my team and I could see the glassy-eyed look of defeat etched on the faces of my teammates. Many of them were on the sideline, down on one knee with their head slumped between their shoulders. The score was fourteen to seventeen. The Titans were ahead by a few points and my team, the Thunderbirds, had a short time to either score a touchdown for the victory or score a field goal so that we could tie the game up and take the battle into overtime.

I stood in the backfield near the twenty-five-yard line waiting for the football to be punted to me. I'd taken Romeo's position and hoped that they wouldn't hit me hard enough to break a bone. I briefly listened to the echoed chants of the Thunderbird cheerleaders. I began to focus on what I had to do, which was to return the football to at least the forty-yard line so that Marlon, our star quarterback, could move the team down the field and take a shot at connecting with a receiver for a touchdown. Pacing back and forth I tried to anticipate the direction in which the Titans' punter would kick the ball to me.

The roar of the crowd reached an earsplitting level as the players lined the field in anticipation of the punt. I glanced up into the stands and noticed that everyone had risen to their feet. I closed my eyes, then took some deep breaths and wiggled my fingers, making sure they functioned in the cold winter air. The last thing I wanted to do was drop the ball and give the Titans a chance to recover it. I briefly fiddled with the tan breathing strip that was on the bridge of my nose, making sure that my sweaty skin hadn't caused the adhesive to come unglued. When I heard the referee blow his whistle, I stopped prancing around, dug my cleats deeper into the grass and waited for the play to unfold.

"Let's go, Mike!" I heard one of my optimistic teammates yelling from the sideline. "This is our time and our championship! They can't stop the Thunderbirds, baby!" I heard the thudding sound of the football being kicked. The punter kicked the ball toward the left side of the field. I quickly moved in that direction and got beneath the ball. It hung in the air for a long time before it came hurling end-over-end toward me.

"Drop it, fool!" I heard one of the Titans yell out as he sped toward me. I tuned him out and remained focused. The ball was about to land in my hands. I fought the urge to take my eyes off it for a moment so that I could see what type of running lane was available, but I knew that any lapse in concentration would be a colossal error. I reached up and plucked the ball out of the air.

The moment my hands secured the ball, I exploded to my right side toward a pack of angry Titans waiting to knock me flat on my back. Fearlessly I rocketed toward them at a blinding speed. My plan was to burst through the cluster of defenders and keep on going. Just before they were about to place their hands on me, I saw an opening to my left and quickly cut in that direction. The running lane was narrow and collapsing quickly. I boomed through the lane before it caved in. I shot down the field like a missile chasing a target.

Out of the corner of my eye, I saw a Titan rushing toward me. I thought for sure I was about to get tackled until Jason, one of my teammates, leveled him. The block provided me with nothing but open field and opportunity, which was all I needed. I willed my legs to turn over more quickly. As I accelerated, I listened to the sound of the wind as it whistled past my ears while I showed everyone just how spectacular my running speed was.

When I crossed the goal line for a touchdown, I tossed the football over my right shoulder and yelled out as loud as I could. I felt strong, invincible and indestructible. I couldn't quell the urge to celebrate, so I began to perform the Soulja Boy dance inside the end zone. My fluid dance moves caused the crowd to scream. A moment later all my teammates surrounded me filled with excitement and renewed energy.

"You did it!" I heard Jason yell out.

"That's right," I growled.

"We're going to win, Mike! This game is about to be over, baby!" Jason shouted as he continually jumped up and down. The roar of the crowd was deafening and the liveliness that was in the air was undeniable. I trotted back over to the bench with my teammates so that the field goal unit could come out and kick for an extra point. I watched from the sidelines as the ball was snapped and then punted perfectly between the uprights. As soon as the ball sailed through them, time ran out.

"We're state champions! Thunderbirds forever!" someone shouted out. We all began chanting the name "Thunderbirds" loud and clear so that the Titans knew exactly who'd won. Our coach tried to calm us down before we were penalized for bad sportsmanship but our jubilation could not be contained. My teammates and I did shake hands with all of the Titan players before heading back to the locker room. As we all jogged toward the locker room, we once again began chanting our team name.

Once inside, we all began retelling the events that had taken place on the field.

"Did you see how Marlon kept the defense confused by looking one way and throwing the ball in the other direction?" asked Steve, one of the defensive linemen.

"Did you guys see how John sacked their quarterback four times? John was tackling him as if he owed him money," laughed another player.

"And when Marlon threw that perfect pass and hit Rick in full stride. Whoa, that was a thing of pure beauty, baby!" said Andrew, one of the wide receivers.

"Okay guys, listen up." Coach Joe, a man with a deep Southern accent, spoke above our loud chatter. "Give me your attention for a moment." It took a second before everyone stopped talking.

"Today, we let everyone know that the Thunderbirds are true champions. I'm so proud of you guys and what you've accomplished. This trophy will sit in the display case as a reminder of what this talented team has achieved." Coach Joe picked up the tall trophy and passed it around so everyone had an opportunity to hold it. "Make sure that you all stay connected with our graduating seniors." He continued. "Laski, Linahan, Panky and Steele. This was the last game for those guys and I can't think of a better way to end their high-school football career. I have the game ball in my hand. I don't know about you guys, but I think the game ball needs to go to Mike Kendall." Everyone in the room began to chant my name which made me feel extra special.

"Mike, you've earned this. All the extra time you've spent in the weight room has really paid off. You've not only earned respect but also you've put fear in the hearts of our opponents. Son, you seem to have developed the speed of Devin Hester, Michael Johnson and Usain Bolt all overnight. Your quickness is mind-blowing. You make sure that you see Coach Miller about joining the track team this spring. If you keep up this pace, you've got an awesome athletic career ahead of you."

"I'll do that," I said proudly.

"The game ball." Coach held it up. "This goes to Mike for saving our you know what!" Everyone howled and screamed at the top of their voices.

"The MVP award for this game goes to our team captain and quarterback, Marlon Hanks. A guy who has demonstrated excellent leadership on and off the field and has led this team to the state championship." Everyone began to howl for Marlon.

"Hang on, guys. Listen up. It's not all about Mike, Marlon and Rick. It's about everyone. You guys are one hell of a unit. You're all winners and champions. Also a quick update on Romeo, he's going to be just fine. What we thought was a broken arm turned out to be a very badly sprained wrist. Now hit the showers, pack your bags and get on the bus so that we can head on home."

Everyone continued to howl with jubilation as we headed toward the showers.

When I exited the locker room, I walked down a long corridor that led to the school bus that would take my teammates and me back home. Just as I was about to board the school bus, I heard someone call my name.

"Michael Earl Kendall, the fastest man on the planet."

I recognized my grandmother's voice right away.

"Grandma," I said dropping my bulky football helmet and gear to move toward her.

"Give me a hug," she said before embracing me tightly. "Oh, look at you. You're getting so strong and muscular," she said as she squeezed my rock-solid arms.

"Well, you know, I've got a few cuts," I said boasting about my physical prowess. "When did you get here? I called you on your cell phone before the game but I got your voice mail. Did you get my message?"

"I got your message. You called me when I was at the veterinarian's office with Smokey."

"How is Smokey doing anyway? Is he still trying to chase down jackrabbits?" I asked.

"Yes, he is, but Smokey can't run them down like he used to. Fact of the matter is that you can probably chase them down quicker than Smokey can." She laughed. "I was starting to worry about that dog because he was walking around the house grumpy and acting like an old cranky man. I took him in for a checkup and learned that he's starting to have joint problems. The vet gave him some medicine for his sore joints and said that he should begin to feel better." Grandmother Katie paused and smiled at me once again. "I saw you run that ball back for a touchdown."

"Did you really?" I asked, excited about the fact that she'd seen me.

"Oh, yes, and you ran like the wind, honey. Once you go into the open field, you outran everyone."

"I made them look like they were walking, didn't I?" I asked boastfully.

"You most certainly did. And I got it all on video."

"For real?" I said super excited. "Oh, you've got to send that to me."

"I will." She knew that I'd flip over the fact that she'd captured my team's performance on video.

"Ooh, I can't wait to post clips of it," I said.

"Well, when I get home, I'll download it and e-mail it to you."

"You remember how to do it, right?" I asked a little concerned that she may not have remembered how to operate her computer or video camera. This day was too important for mistakes.

"Of course I do. I'm not one of these elderly people who is afraid of technology. You know, I'm on a committee at church that teaches grandparents how to use a computer."

"Okay. I'll give you that. You've never been one to allow anything to slow you down."

"No I haven't. I'm still as a sharp as surgeon's blade." She laughed at her own joke. "Well run along and get on the bus before they leave you. Enjoy your time with the team. I just wanted to tell you how proud I was of you and to let you know that I'd made it to see you and the team win."

"Thank you," I said and then gave her a kiss before I picked up my equipment and rushed through the doors of the bus.

As I headed to one of the seats in the rear, I could tell my teammates were all still excited by our victory. Once the bus got on the highway, I located my cell phone and called home.

"Hello," I heard Keysha answer the phone.

"What's up, son?" I asked as I glanced out the window at the passing vehicles. Several of the cars had the Thunderbirds banner attached to their antennas.

"Mike, stop calling me *son*. How many times do I have to tell you that?" Keysha was being her usual whiny self.

"Where's Mom?" I asked.

"In her skin," Keysha answered me sarcastically.

"You know what, stop screwing around, Keysha, and put her on the phone." I wasn't in the mood to play around with her.

"Make me," she said defiantly.

"Girl, I swear I'll make you regret the day you were born if you don't put her on the phone," I said through gritted teeth. I slapped the back of the seat in front of me out of annoyance.

"I would put her on but she's not here," Keysha said.

"Where is she at?" I asked wondering why my mom wasn't at home.

"I don't know. It's not my turn to watch her," Keysha's tone was nasty.

"Why are your panties all in a knot?"

"Shut up, Mike!" Keysha snapped.

"Shut doesn't go up! Prices do. And if you keep flapping your lips I'm going to— Hello? Hello? Ooh, I swear that girl is going to drive me insane," I said realizing that Keysha had hung up on me. I called my mother on her cell phone. It rang a few times before she picked it up.

"Hey, Mom," I greeted her.

"Hey. How did the game go? Did you guys win?" she asked.

"Yeah, and you should've seen me. I scored the winning touchdown. I ran the ball back seventy-five yards," I stated, hoping to impress her with what I'd done as well as make her proud of me.

"Wow! That's wonderful. I'm so sorry that I missed your game. I just feel horrible about it. But there was no way I could get out of attending the church board meeting. I know your father feels the same way but he had a sales conference this weekend."

"It's cool. Grandmother Katie came to the game and videotaped everything. So we'll get to sit down and watch it together. Where are you?" I asked.

"I'm on my way home from the long board meeting. I was hoping that I'd still have time to run some of my normal Saturday afternoon errands but that will just have to wait until Sunday. Now remind me, what time will the bus be back at the school so that I can pick you up?"

"Around 11:30 p.m. I can get a ride home from Marlon I think. That way you don't have to come back out in the cold. Hold on a second." I pressed the Mute button on my cell phone.

"Yo, Marlon," I called out as I searched the bus for my friend.

"Yeah," I heard his voice answer me from behind. I turned to look at him. He was sitting with another teammate talking and laughing.

"Can I get a ride home with you?" I asked.

"What? Do I look like a cab service to you, man?" he joked.

"Come on, man, seriously. Can I catch a ride back to the crib with you?" I asked again.

"Yeah. I got you," Marlon said. "No problem."

"Mom?" I spoke back into the phone. When I didn't get a response I remembered that I'd pressed the Mute button.

"Mom, are you there?" I asked once I'd taken her off hold.

"Yes, I'm here," she answered.

"Don't worry about coming to pick me up. Marlon is going to give me a ride back."

"Are you sure? I'll come pick you up. I don't mind," she said.

"Mom, it's okay. You don't have to pick me up and drop me off all the time." I paused. "I can't wait to get my driver's license so that I can drive myself around."

"One step at a time, Mike. You'll be driving soon enough." I could hear a bit of uneasiness in her voice.

"I'll be turning fifteen and getting my permit soon. Then before you know it, I'll have my driver's license. Once I get my license, I'm going to start looking for a car. You and dad are still going to get me a car when I get my driver's license, right?"

"We'll see," she said but she didn't sound very certain.

"I'm for real, Mom. We can get a good deal on a used car for about ten thousand dollars. Just think. If I had my own wheels, you wouldn't have to drive me around all the time. I could run some of your errands for you and—"

"Mike, slow down. You're getting way ahead of yourself. Besides, we're going to have to reevaluate the idea of you getting a car. With Keysha living with us now and being of driving age already, we'll have to make some adjustments. You guys may have to share a car."

"No way! I don't want to drive around in some girlie car. She'll probably want some stupid color like pink. I want a red Mustang. I know you're not thinking about putting Keysha before me!" I'd just about lost it. "I was here first, remember. *I'm* your son. Keysha shouldn't get a car before me or even have a say in what car I get. Keysha probably doesn't know a thing about cars and I do. Besides, she could get into trouble if she had a car. You know that trouble follows her around like a stray dog."

"Mike, I didn't say that she was getting a car. All I

said was that your father and I are discussing what would be best."

"What's going on with Keysha anyway?" I asked. "When I called earlier she was tripping on the phone."

There was a long moment of silence before my mother said anything. I instinctively knew that something was up. "Keysha is just in a strange place right now." I could tell that she wanted to say more but she held on to her thoughts.

"Ever since that girl moved in with us she's had nothing but trouble. I don't think that anything will ever go right in her life," I said completely convinced that Keysha was some type of drama magnet.

"Mike, don't say that. Being sarcastic isn't going to help." My mother was warning me that I was skating on thin ice with my criticism of Keysha.

"Why are you choosing her over me?" I asked. I seriously felt disregarded.

"I'm not choosing her over you, honey," she said defensively.

"Well, it feels like it." I paused in thought for a moment. "I don't know how much more of Keysha I can take. I don't want to deal with any more of her problems. At first, it was cool trying to help, but now her tragic issues are just annoying."

"I can understand how you feel but we just have to work together in order to get through this latest crisis with Keysha. Her mother showing up the way she did was difficult for her."

I was silent for a long moment because I didn't want my mother dealing with Keysha anymore. I wanted her to focus on my needs and me. "Yeah, whatever," I uttered.

"Don't be like that, Mike," she said softly. "I'll see you when you get home. We'll talk some more then. Oh, and Mike?"

"Yeah?"

"Congratulations on winning the state championship. I'm proud of you," she said.

I don't know if she heard my thank-you before I hung up the phone.

three

KEYSHA
Saturday, November 3rd

yesterday, when Wesley said that he and his dad would be moving I felt as if he was holding my head underwater against my will. I couldn't breathe and I gasped for air.

"Keysha? Are you okay?" he asked as he patted my back. "Are you choking on something?"

"No. I just need to get inside the house and sit down," I said as I caught his gaze for a moment. After seeing the concern in his eyes, I said, "Let's go. I'll be okay." Wesley walked me the rest of the way home and when we arrived I invited him inside. Wesley sat on the sofa in the family room while I went to get us both a soda from the kitchen.

"Where are the folks?" he asked.

"Barbara's at a board meeting, Jordan's at a sales conference and Mike is at his football game. It's okay. No one will be home for a while," I said reassuring him.

"Okay, cool," he said as he tried to relax a little.

"You know, you can't leave!" I said as I filled his glass with ice cubes and a Pepsi drink trying to keep the panic from my voice.

"I don't have a choice, Keysha. I wish that I didn't have to leave but there is just nothing I can do."

"Where are you and you dad moving to?" I asked as I handed him his drink. When he didn't answer right away, I moved over to the stereo and turned it on. I needed to play some music in order to lighten the tension in the room.

"You don't want to know," Wesley answered as he took a sip of his drink.

"Come on, tell me. I can handle it," I said as I inhaled deeply.

"Indianapolis, Indiana," Wesley answered.

"Indianapolis—that's like two hours away from here. How are we going to see each other?" I snapped.

"I don't know, Keysha. My dad and I are going to live with my grandmother until the house is fixed and he's healed."

"Well," I paused in thought for a moment. "You guys can't move that far away. What about follow-up visits to his doctor? What are you guys going to do about that?"

"The hospital has recommended a burn specialist down in Indianapolis. They've already begun duplicating my dad's medical records so that we can take them with us."

"When are you leaving?" I said, feeling my throat begin to close with emotion.

Wesley stood up and walked over to me and placed his hands on my shoulders. He then began lightly stroking my right cheek to comfort me. "We'll be leaving in about a week," he said softly.

"What about school? You just came back and you're just starting to turn your grades around. Did your dad consider that the move might set you back?" I asked.

"I promised him that I wouldn't mess up again. I promised him that I'd stay focused on what I needed to do and not fall behind again at my new school."

"This isn't fair!" I cried stepping away from him.

"Keysha." Wesley stood behind me and wrapped his arms around me. He kissed the side of my neck. "Don't make this any harder than it already is," Wesley whispered in my ear. He turned me around to face him. "You know that I can't breathe without you." Wesley tilted my chin up and gazed deeply into my eyes. I felt goose bumps rise up on my skin.

"What are you doing to me?" I asked even though the answer to my question was shining brightly in his eyes. Wesley craned his neck and paused just before kissing me. His kiss once again made me feel weak and I melted like butter on a warm stove.

"Ooh," I cooed as I pulled myself away from him. "This could lead to trouble," I warned him.

"Trouble? I'm not afraid of trouble. I believe that I've proven that to you already," Wesley said as he kissed me once again. And he was right. Wesley helped prove Liz Lloyd planted drugs in my locker, and now she was in jail, instead of me. I surrendered to his second kiss and listened as our breathing patterns synchronized.

"You know what I mean," I finally said breaking away from him once again. "This could lead to other things that could—"

"Shh," he said. "Don't think right now. Let's have this moment with each other because it may be a long time before we get another chance to have a moment like this. All I want to do is hold you, dance with you and feel your heart close to mine."

"How do you do that?" I asked.

"Do what?"

"You have a way with words, Wesley. You're poetic." I smiled.

"I write poetry from time to time. I even wrote a poem about you once. But I was just being goofy," he confessed.

"You wrote a poem about me and you haven't let me read it? What's up with that?" I asked feeling almost betrayed that he had a part of him that he hadn't shared with me.

"It's nothing really. I was just writing down some of my thoughts." Wesley laughed a little.

"I want to read it," I said, sweeping my thumb lightly across his bottom lip. "Will you let me read some of your writing?" I whispered.

"Yeah," Wesley uttered as his bottom lip quivered a little.

That was the first time that I'd ever seen a boy's lip do that. I looked into Wesley's eyes once again and saw the desire that had flooded them. And I wanted him, too. It was at that moment I realized that Wesley and I were slowly seducing each other with tender love and that frightened me because it was all too easy for me to submit to him. "You should go, Wesley," I said reluctantly stepping away from him.

"What?" I could hear the disappointment and edginess in his voice. I knew that I'd gotten him excited and hot.

"I think you should go," I said, my tone uncertain to my own ears. Wesley picked up on my uneasiness.

"Did I do something wrong?" he asked.

"No," I assured him.

"Then what is it?" He pressed. I didn't blame him for wanting to know why I'd suddenly done a 180-degree turn on him.

"I forgot that Jordan said he may be coming home early," I lied.

"Why do I get the feeling that you're not telling me the truth, Keysha?" Wesley asked.

"It *is* the truth. Jordan could come home at any moment and although he likes you, he's not going to be too thrilled with the idea of us being all alone. Plus, I'm starting to itch again," I added.

"Oh," Wesley answered. "By the way, I'm not trying to put any pressure or anything on you, Keysha. I was just going with the flow of the moment."

"I understand," I said, happy to see that I'd successfully

changed the direction we were headed in. I took Wesley by the hand and walked him to door.

"Call me when you get home," I said as I held the door open for him.

"Okay." He paused before stepping out into the cold. "Look, it's snowing," he said. I glanced outside and saw snowflakes billowing down from the heavens. "It always looks so pretty when it first falls," I said wistfully.

"I hate snow," Wesley whined. "I hate having to shovel it and I hate having to walk to school in it because it gets in my shoes, wets up my socks and turns my toes into mini popsicles."

"It's not snowing that hard," I said and then thought about Wesley's ability to keep warm on a cold night like the one that was ahead of us.

"Are you keeping warm in that cold house of yours?" I asked suddenly feeling bad for putting him out.

"My space heater does a good job, but I will not be sleeping in the house tonight because my grandmother is here and she's gotten a hotel room for us. She's at the hospital now. I'm going to stop by my house for a moment and pack some clothes before calling her to come pick me up. Hey, do you want to come back to my house for a little while? You could help me pack and meet my grandmother when she arrives."

"Not this time, Wesley. Maybe next time." I said as I smiled at him. Wesley smiled back and then turned to head home. I closed the door and exhaled loudly. I was relieved and proud of myself for not acting on my impulses.

four

MIKE
Sunday, November 4th

"MIKE," I heard my mother call out my name from the bottom of the staircase. I was in my bed barely awake. I was hoping that she didn't really want or need me for anything. "Mike!" she yelled out my name again, this time with more authority.

"Yeah," I responded, still feeling very groggy.

"Get up and get dressed for church," she commanded.

"Mom, I'm still tired from yesterday's game. Can't I just sleep in this morning?" I complained.

"No! Get up and get dressed," she said.

I grumbled and turned over deciding that I needed to sleep for a few more minutes. My bed was so comfortable and warm. The last thing I wanted to do was throw back the covers and feel a rush of cool air.

"Mike!" I heard my mother call out my name once again.

"Yeah," I answered her.

"Are you up?"

"Yeah, I'm up," I said.

"No, you're not. You're still in the bed. Now, get up! I woke you up a half hour ago. Now get out of that bed and let me hear some water running!"

"Okay," I said as I tossed back the covers, placed my bare feet on the cold floor and walked toward the bathroom. I turned on the faucet so that she knew I was actually up.

"Dang, it's cold," I grumbled as I tried to rub away the goose bumps on my skin. I shuffled over to the bathroom window and glanced outside, noticing that there was a light dusting of snow on the ground. I then turned on the heat lamp to help warm up the bathroom. I grabbed a towel from the linen cabinet and was about to wash my face but couldn't because the countertop was covered with Keysha's skin- and hair-care products.

"This girl gets on my nerves," I said angrily. "Keysha!" I shouted out her name as I stepped out of the bathroom and marched toward her room. Her door was closed. I didn't bother to knock. I just opened the door because I was irritated.

"Girl, get in there and clean up that mess you left in the bathroom!" I snapped at her.

"Who in the world do you think you're yelling at?" Keysha barked back at me. "And how dare you fling my door open without knocking." She was fully dressed for church and sitting on the edge of her bed with her cellular phone glued to her ear.

"Get off the phone and handle that mess you left in the bathroom." I pointed my finger toward the direction of the bathroom.

"Wesley, let me call you back in a minute," Keysha said and then hung up the phone. "First of all, you need to get your attitude in order. You don't be coming up in here acting like you all big and bad, Mike."

"Just go and do what I told you to do," I said, asserting my masculinity. "I'm tired of you hogging up all the countertop space. Now, go handle that mess so I can do what I need to do."

"I don't have to do anything except stay black and die!" Keysha folded her arms across her chest and refused to move.

"Oh, you want to fight with me? You'd better think about that first." I warned her. "And what the heck is wrong with your skin? Why does it look like you have some kind of disease?"

"Shut up! I don't have a disease. I'm just having an allergic reaction to something. Barbara has already scheduled an appointment with a doctor for me."

"Barbara has already scheduled an appointment with the doctor for me." I mocked. I was weary of her relationship with my mother. "Well whatever you have, keep your fleas to yourself! Now go do what I told you," I barked at her.

"Boy! You're not tough. You may be more muscular but underneath all of that, you're still a wimp who'll start crying for your mama at the first sign of danger. So go on. Call Jordan or Barbara so they can come to your rescue before I beat you down."

Keysha trapped my gaze. I couldn't believe that she knew that my next move was to call my mother to come and handle her. "Go on, little boy. Call for yo mama." Keysha continued to antagonize me.

"I'm not a little boy. I'm a man and I don't need my mother to fight my battles for me. Now either you get in there and clean that mess up or you and I are going to make some furniture move up in here and I don't care what the consequences are!" I threatened through clenched teeth. At any moment I was ready to do anything to wipe the snug look off her face.

Keysha searched my eyes and saw that I was dead serious about what I'd said. "Okay," Keysha said softly as she bowed to my will. She headed toward the bathroom but I was blocking her path. "Are you going to move so that I can go take care of that? Big Mike?"

I liked the sound of that. "Big Mike." It seemed to fit with how I felt. I was about to turn fifteen and feeling more like a man than I'd ever felt before. I stepped aside and allowed her to pass. I turned and watched Keysha as she entered our shared bathroom and cleaned up the mess she'd left.

Once she was done, she exited the bathroom and said, "You can get in there now, Big Mike," and then walked down the stairs.

"Good," I said as I entered the bathroom so that I could prepare for church.

After I'd taken a hot shower, the bathroom was filled with warm white steam. I stepped over to the mirror, took a dry cloth, placed it against the mirror and moved my hand in a circular motion wiping away the mist so that I could see myself.

Keysha was right, I thought to myself. I'd put on about fifteen pounds of extra muscle. My triceps and biceps were noticeably bigger. My abs looked as if they'd been chiseled from stone, and my chest and shoulders were broader and bulkier. I raised my arms up, curled my fingers into fists and flexed my biceps as tightly as I could.

"Yeah," I growled at my reflection enjoying the intensity of my might and muscular power. "If I had a few tattoos, the girls would be all over this." I drummed my right fist against my chest a few times. I turned on a small radio that was in the bathroom and smiled at myself feeling a newfound confidence. I finished up in the bathroom, got dressed and then headed downstairs just as everyone was about to leave.

"What's up, Jordan?" I said to my father as I entered the room.

"You're lucky that I didn't have to come upstairs to pull you out of the mirror, Mike." My father wasn't pleased that I'd taken so long to get dressed. For a moment I tried to figure out how he'd known that I was standing in front of the mirror admiring myself.

"I don't feel like going to church anyway. I don't see why I have to go," I complained. "I'd really rather do something else with my time."

"Well you're going whether you like it or not, mister!" Jordan snapped at me.

"What?" I glared at him. I suddenly felt like it was national pick-on-Mike day.

"Get your attitude in check, boy!" Jordan was all over me and I didn't understand why.

"Jesus, have a coronary, why don't you," I mumbled beneath my breath.

"You have something to say Mike?" Jordan's voice was filled with confrontation.

"No," I answered as I walked past him. I headed out the door and toward the garage so that I could get in the car, plug up my iPod and tune everyone out. I was tired of everyone riding my back for the littlest things. I swear, ever since Keysha arrived, I was treated like the stepchild instead of her. At first, my Mom was on my side and was just as suspicious of Keysha as I was, but then she flipped the script on me, befriended her and turned against me. Suddenly, Keysha could do no wrong in her eyes. Now, my dad, Jordan, was all over me for the smallest things. I felt as if he was searching for any reason to chew me out. He hadn't said or even asked me about how I did at the football game. One of these days, he's going to push me too hard and it's going to be on.

I got in the car, put my seat belt on, jacked in my iPod player and slumped down in the seat. I stared out the window as we drove out of the driveway down the street. A lot of time had passed since my parents and I had been to church. In fact, now that I think about it, the last time we went was just before Keysha came to live with us. Before that she lived briefly in a group home when her mom wound up behind bars. I didn't mind going to church when it was just mom, my dad and me. Now it was different, especially with Keysha tagging along.

I knew the moment we'd entered the church people who'd heard and read about all of the drama with Keysha's court case would start asking questions about the details and how the family had beaten the case. Keysha would without a doubt garner all of the attention and that fact alone irked me.

When we arrived at church, Jordan let us out at the door and then went to park the car. I was grooving to my music as I walked into the church lobby. Then out of nowhere, my mom pinched and twisted my skin.

"Ouch!" I shouted. "What did you do that for?" I hollered at her. My mom gave me an evil look.

"Turn off the iPod music while you're in church. What's gotten into you lately?" She glared at me as if she didn't know me.

I huffed, sighed and then cut my eyes at her. "Nothing," I said as I turned off my music, pulled out my earplugs and wrapped the wires around the iPod player. I stuffed my hands in my pockets and stood still. That seemed to be the only thing I could do without getting into trouble.

"Why are you all twisted?" Keysha asked me.

"Mind your own business, itchy," I snarled.

"You must be on your period!" she laughed at me, then turned toward Barbara who had struck up a conversation with one of the church trustees. Keysha stood at her side and waited to be introduced. My mom finally draped her arm around her and introduced her as her daughter.

"Whatever," I uttered disapprovingly. I was about to just go and grab a seat but I felt someone tap me on the shoulder. I turned around and saw Sabrina Collins, a girl that I knew from both church and school. Sabrina and I were the same age although she was older than me by a few months. I'd always known her as a chubby tomboy with a goofy smile, unruly hair that needed a perm, braces, thick eyeglasses and bad skin. But Sabrina looked nothing like she did when I last saw her. She seemed to have blossomed overnight. Her braces had been removed and her skin had definitely cleared up. She'd gotten a perm and her hair was styled asymmetrically the way Rihanna the singer likes to wear her hair. Sabrina had full cheeks, a round face and a body that had a lot of sexy curves from what I could tell through her church clothes.

"Mike, is that you?" she asked.

"Yeah," I said smiling at her.

"You don't look anything like you used to," she said.

"Girl, I know you're not tripping like that. You're like a dang Transformer. There's more to you than what meets the eye," I said, laughing as I continued to check her out on the sly.

"You're all muscular now," she said as she gripped my arm. "You look good. You look more manly and more mature," she said.

I licked my lips and nodded my head. *Finally*. A girl that recognizes all of my hard work. "Yeah. That's right. I've got it going on a little bit these days. But you're looking pretty hot yourself. I mean you were okay-looking before," I lied. "But now, wow! You've lost— I mean, you look like a million bucks. Turn around. Let me take all of you in." Sabrina slowly turned so I could really see her. My eyes were all over her and it was at a time like this that I wished for X-ray vision.

"Well, thank you. I try." A broad grin broke out on her face revealing even, white teeth.

"Where have you been? I haven't seen you around school at all," I asked.

"Mike, you pretty much put some distance between you and me after my eleventh birthday party," she said.

"What are you talking about?" I asked, not sure of what she meant.

"Come on, Mike, don't act as if you don't remember what happened."

"Oh, that. That was four years ago, Sabrina."

"It may have been, but I remember it very well. I told you that I liked you in front of everyone and kissed you on the cheek and the way you reacted embarrassed me."

"That was a long time ago. Why do you want to bring up old stuff?" I asked hoping she'd just drop the conversation.

"Because you made me feel horrible for liking you. You

yelled at me and told me to never touch you again," Sabrina recalled.

I could tell she was still searching for an explanation or at least an apology, so I offered one. "I'm sorry for making you feel bad. I was a different person at that time. But you can certainly kiss me on the cheek now. There is no doubt about it. I wouldn't mind it at all," I said, hoping that I'd won her over.

"Well, you still are very cute to me," she admitted.

"So, what's up with you? You got a man or what?" I asked feeling that it was the perfect time to pimp up and put some serious moves on her.

"Well, there is this guy that I've liked for a very long time. But he doesn't notice me."

"How could anyone not notice you?" I said utterly shocked that she didn't have a gang of guys trying to get with her.

"I don't know, Mike, you tell me. Why haven't you noticed me at school?" she captured my gaze and held it.

For a moment, I was completely speechless.

"You'd better start noticing what's in front of you, Mike, and stop letting your wicked stepsister occupy all of your time with her drama."

"Sho you right!" I said feeling myself buzzing with lustful energy. I was about to say something very mannish but I caught my words before they fell out of my mouth when I saw Sabrina's dad and Jordan approaching.

"Look, I'll holla at you later. Your dad's coming," I informed her.

"Oh," she said and immediately stopped smiling at me.

"So do you have an e-mail address, MySpace page or a cell phone number so that we can talk?"

"My father would have a fit if I gave my cell phone number to you," said Sabrina.

"Oh. It's like that. He doesn't want you dating?" I asked.

"No. I can't date until I'm eighteen according to him," she said.

"Oh, that's just dumb," I said looking over her shoulder again at her father who seemed to be searching the crowd of churchgoers.

"I think he's looking for you now," I said.

"He probably is. Look, I sing in the choir. I'm doing a solo today. Make sure you listen."

"I will."

"I'll see you around, okay?" she said before turning to walk away from me. I couldn't help but study the curves of her banging body.

"Who are you looking at so hard?" Jordan asked as he approached me.

"No one," I said and turned back to face Keysha and my mother who were chatting it up with some women. They appeared to be talking about some home remedies for Keysha's skin.

Turning back to Jordan, I said, "What's up with Keysha and her grossed-out-looking skin? We should call up a Hollywood producer and tell him that we have the perfect creature for the next blockbuster horror film. She looks like one of those dead creatures from that movie *Resident Evil.* I wouldn't be surprised if she started foaming at the mouth and growling. She probably needs to be quarantined so that she doesn't infect everyone."

"Mike! What has gotten into you?" Jordan smacked me on the chest with the back of his hand. My eyes immediately met his and we locked our gaze upon each other. "You don't talk about your sister like that. The next time you say something that mean-spirited about her you and I are going to get into it." Jordan wasn't happy but neither was I. I refused to break eye contact with him. "Have I made myself clear?" Jordan poked me in the chest a few times with his index finger. His thumps didn't hurt me one bit but I could tell that he thought they had.

"I hear you," I answered him, still refusing to break eye contact.

"Is there something going on with you, Mike? You've been behaving very odd lately," Jordan asked. I cut my eyes at him because he honestly didn't have a clue. At that moment I heard Marlon call out my name. I turned and saw him maneuvering his way through the crowd of people toward me.

"Dude, have you seen the newspaper?" he asked.

"No?"

"Here, take a look. There's a huge photo of you running the ball back for a touchdown." Marlon opened the newspaper and showed me the photo. Below the photo of me sprinting down the field were the words *Mike "The Sonic Boom" Kendall Electrified the Crowd When He*

Ran Seventy-five Yards for a Touchdown to Clinch the State Championship for the Thunderbirds.

"Did you see it, Mr. Kendall?" asked Marlon as he showed the newspaper to my father.

"I didn't know. I forgot all about the game," Jordan said.

"That's because you're so busy worrying about a skin rash," I said condescendingly. My dad allowed my comment to slide for the moment.

"Mike, I'm proud of you," he said, but at that point it was too late and his last-minute words held no real value to me.

"I'm going to go sit with Marlon. Is that okay?" I asked.

"Yeah," Jordan said. "Meet us out here at the end of service." I could tell that my dad wanted to know more details about the game, but I didn't feel like talking to him anymore.

"Come on, Marlon. Let's go find a seat," I said and followed him into the sanctuary.

five

KEYSHA
Sunday, November 4th

when I arrived home from church on Sunday, I headed directly to my bedroom so that I could grab my cell phone off my dresser and call Wesley. Barbara and Jordan insisted that Mike and I leave our cellular phones at home because they didn't want us sending text messages while we were in church. When I looked at my phone, I noticed that I'd received several text messages from Wesley asking me to call him right away. I even noticed that I had a voice mail message that I assumed was from him, too. I smiled, because I was happy to learn that Wesley had been thinking about me.

We'd made plans to see each other again today and talk about how we were going to keep in touch. I'd even planned on going over to meet his grandmother and help them pack. I opened my closet door and pulled out a pair of blue jeans, a sweater and my gym shoes. I tossed my outfit on the bed to make sure that I liked what I'd picked. The sweater wasn't moving me, so I decided to see what else I had in the closet that I could wear. I wanted to make sure that I had on something that Wesley would remember. As I rambled through my closet, I received another text message from Wesley saying good-bye.

"Good-bye!" I said aloud. I stepped out of my closet, sat on the edge of my bed and called him.

"Hey, babe," I greeted him. "I just got your text message. What's up?" I asked.

"What took you so long to call me back?" he asked. I could hear a little uneasiness in his voice.

"I went to church this morning and I didn't have my phone with me."

"Oh," Wesley said with a big sigh.

"Are you okay? Is something wrong? And what's up with this good-bye text message?" A feeling of panic gripped me.

"I'm gone, Keysha. I'm already on the road leaving town with my dad and grandmother."

"What?" I yelled into the phone. "What are you talking about? We had plans this afternoon."

"The plans changed. My grandmother and I came to the house this morning, packed up everything and then came to get my dad from the hospital. They released him early and my grandmother wanted to get back right away." Wesley kept on talking but I wasn't really listening to him because I felt my heart sinking.

"That's not fair!" I said as a teardrop ran down my cheek. Wesley was silent. "How could you do this to me?" I snapped at him.

"Keysha, I didn't have a choice. I had to leave with them. We're in the car driving now," he said in a defeated tone.

"Can they hear you talking on the phone?" I asked.

"My dad is asleep but my grandmother knows that I'm on the phone," Wesley explained.

"Well tell her that I said that it's not fair that you left without saying good-bye to me!" I couldn't control the tears streaming from my eyes.

"I'm sorry," Wesley said, his voice full of regret.

"This isn't right," I said as I began pacing back and forth. "This doesn't make any sense. Why would she make you leave without saying good-bye to your friends? Doesn't she realize how important your friends are? Didn't she want to at least meet me? What was the big rush?" I asked, smearing away the steady stream of tears running down my cheeks.

"I don't know the answers to all of those questions. She just wanted to get back as soon as possible," Wesley said, but his words offered me little comfort.

"I'm going crazy, Wesley," I said, and I continued to pace the floor. "How am I going to deal with the people at school? How am I going to function without you around?" I asked.

"I know it's going to be hard, but I'm not at any picnic here either. I have to go to another school yet again with a bunch of kids I don't know. This isn't going to be easy for me either, Keysha," Wesley argued.

"When are you coming back?" I asked.

"I don't know yet," he paused for a moment, and in the background I heard his grandmother demand that he get off of the phone.

"What the hell?" I shouted into the phone. "You can't even have a conversation while she's driving?"

"Keysha, let me call you back," Wesley said.

"Why is she being so mean? I didn't do anything to her. She's never even met me and she doesn't like me. What kind of sense does that make?"

"Wesley, I'm not going to ask you to get off the phone again. Tell that fast little girl that the world isn't coming to an end and you'll have to call her later," I heard his grandmother say.

"Keysha, I promise. I'll call you as soon as I get settled," Wesley whispered.

"Who is she calling fast? What did you tell her, Wesley?" I demanded.

"I didn't say anything." Wesley was trying to end the conversation. I had no choice but to let him go.

"Promise you'll call?" I asked, conceding to the fact that I didn't know when or where I'd see Wesley again.

"I will," he said and then said his final good-bye. When I hung up the phone, I crashed onto my bed, placed my face in my pillow and cried so hard that I gave myself a massive headache.

A while later, once the tears had stopped flowing, I

decided to find some Tylenol tablets for my headache. I exited my bedroom and ran into Mike who was coming up the stairs carrying a load of his laundry.

"Whoa!" he looked at me with horror in his eyes. "Get back, you beast. Crawl back into your cave!" Mike teased. I gave him an evil look and then offered up my middle finger.

I went into the bathroom and slammed the door shut. I sat on the edge of the bathtub, placed my face in my hands and cried some more. When I was done, I rubbed my fingers though my hair and was mortified when I saw strands of my hair twisted around my fingers. I stood on my feet and looked at myself in the mirror. My eyes were red and swollen from crying, my hair was tangled up one side and branching out on the other. At that moment, I began scratching my arms uncontrollably. When I looked at my skin, there were red welts all over it.

"What's happening to me?" I whispered to my reflection hoping to find an answer to my question. I opened the medicine cabinet and found the bottle of Tylenol tablets. Just as I was about to take two, there was a loud knock on the door.

"Hey, Keysha, guess who just pulled into the driveway?" Mike asked.

"Leave me alone, Mike. You don't want to mess with me right now," I yelled.

"No. I'm for real. Guess who just pulled into the driveway?" he asked again, wanting me to play his little riddle game.

"I said leave me alone! Why can't you do that?" He was so annoying.

"Hey, I'm just trying to inform you that your ghetto mother is back."

I swore my heart stopped beating for a moment. I glanced out the bathroom window and, sure enough, I saw my mother getting out of a car with Simon. I immediately closed the window shade and placed my hand over my heart as I tried to slow my breathing. I searched my mind trying to find a reason for my mother's return.

Something must be going on, I told myself. But what? I rubbed my fingers through my hair once again and more hair came out. "Oh no!"

"I'm for real, Keysha. Your mother is here. Aren't you going to go down and see what she wants?" Mike asked. He sounded happy that Justine had returned. I took a deep breath, stood and willed myself to open the bathroom door.

"Damn, girl! You look worse now than you did before. Is the mirror broke, too? It's got to be at least cracked or something," Mike was relentless in his criticism of my appearance. I didn't respond to his nasty comment. I could only glare at him. I walked into my room to search for a scarf to wrap up my head with Mike trailing behind.

"Well, it's obvious that you're having a bad hair day and a—"

"That's it, Mike!" I felt myself snap. Grabbing a pair of curling irons that were atop my dresser I waved them in front of his face. "Say one more word to me and I'll crack your skull open with this!"

"I'm not—" Mike couldn't even finish his sentence before I flung the curling iron at his head. Mike barely dodged the flying object.

"Keysha, have you lost your ever-loving mind!" Mike yelled at me. I was about to pick up something else and throw it at him, but I heard Barbara call my name from the bottom of the staircase.

"Keysha, come on down here, please," Barbara summoned.

"Your mother wants to see you," Mike sang. I didn't bother to tie my hair up, I just went downstairs. I heard the voices of Jordan, Barbara and my mother coming from the family room. I could tell that there was a rather nasty argument going. I waited in the kitchen out of their line of sight and eavesdropped to find out what was going on.

"Justine, there is really no reason for you to continue coming around. Keysha is being taken care of. She now has a strong family that loves and supports her. You can go and live your life anyway you see fit. You're not responsible for her any longer," I heard Jordan say.

"So what are you trying to say? You don't want your neighbors to know that I'm Keysha's biological mother? You're just going to act as if I don't exist? Is that it?" I could tell that my mother was offended by Jordan's blunt remarks.

"You may be her biological mother but you certainly were not a good provider for her," Jordan fired back.

"I am a good mother, and I was a damn good provider

when she lived with me. I did everything I could for that girl. I may not have had a lot of money but I made a way out of no way." My mother's short fuse and quick temper were about to explode.

"That's not what I've heard," Jordan shot back, unmoved by her anger. I could tell that he was restraining himself and attempting to be as civil as possible.

"Well, I don't know what lies you've heard. But I know that I was a damn good mother to my baby." Justine's voice boomed throughout the room.

"You know good and well that Keysha's life would have been much better than what it was had I known you'd given birth to a child of mine." Jordan was beginning to lose his temper.

"Don't try to twist this around so that I look like the bad person. I've raised that girl for sixteen years by myself without any help from you," Justine snapped.

"You know what. Let's cut to the chase here. Why are you at my house? I've already told you that there is no need for you to come around." I could tell that Jordan was ready to put Justine out of the house. There was a long moment of silence before Justine spoke.

"Since I'm out of jail I'm working on putting my life back together and I think it's time for Keysha to come back home with me." Justine said with absolute conviction. Jordan released a loud and cynical laugh.

"Let me break the facts of the matter down to you. When I met you the only reason you wanted to hook up with me was to steal money from me. You're a drug abuser. You're a liar and a con artist. You wouldn't even buy Keysha clothes or school supplies. You encouraged her to become a teenage mother and you left her home alone for days on end without food or money. If that's your definition of being a good mother who is doing the best that she can then you're certainly a sorry excuse for a parent. I swear, there should be a law preventing women like you from having children," Jordan spat.

"Okay that's enough!" I heard Barbara interrupt them. "Justine, you've just about worn out your welcome here. I'm trying to be optimistic here but my patience is very thin right now."

"I'm not leaving until we talk about replacing the welfare check that I was getting when Keysha lived with me. I know that somebody in here has to be getting some type of government check for her, and I want my cut!" Justine came right out and said exactly what she'd come there for.

"You have go to be kidding me," I heard Jordan say. I could hear the disbelief in his voice. "I don't believe you traveled all the way out here because you feel that someone is taking your government check." Jordan started laughing at my mother again.

"You mean to tell me that there isn't any type of check coming into this house for Keysha at all?" Justine asked once more just to be clear.

"What part of no don't you understand, the *N* or the *O?*" Jordan asked mockingly.

"Then somebody needs to be getting something for her. I could work the system and make it beneficial for all of us. I'll even share my government Link Card with you so that you can get a portion of your groceries for free. All you have to do is let me get visitation rights and I'll take care of the rest." Justine thought that she'd just offered Jordan and Barbara a perfect proposal that they'd jump at.

"No. I'm not going to give you visitation rights!" Jordan snapped out on my mother.

"Well then I'm going to work with my social worker and take you to court. You can't keep me from seeing my daughter!" I heard Justine scream. At that moment I decided that I'd heard enough of their madness and entered the family room. Upon my entrance, everyone stopped their bickering and focused their attention on me.

A look of horror washed over Justine's face before she screamed, "What have you done to my baby? Why is she looking like that? I'm going to bring up abuse charges on you!"

Immediately I became self-conscious about my appearance and a feeling of nausea clouded my stomach. I whirled around to run back upstairs, but my head suddenly felt very light and the room began to spin around. I had to lean against the wall in order to keep myself from collapsing to the floor.

SIX

MIKE
Sunday, November 4th

I was happy that I was the only one in the house. Jordan had once again kicked out cousin Simon and Justine. Once Keysha pulled her now-infamous fainting act, my mom and dad decided that they couldn't wait another day before taking Keysha to see a doctor. So once she was revived, they took her to the emergency room to get checked out. Being alone in the house was so cool because I didn't have to put up with everybody dealing with Keysha's drama. I swear, before she came, life was truly good. I tried being understanding of her tragic life but enough is enough.

I decided to go to the workout room and pump some iron as well as blow off some steam. When I got to the weight room above the garage, I turned on the radio and got pumped when the new hit song by Nelly began blaring through the speakers. I bounced my head to the rhythm of the music and lip-synched along with the words. I then moved over to a small wooden cabinet positioned just below the giant mural of Muhammad Ali and picked up my workout log. I'd planned to do a routine designed to build muscle mass. Once I looked at the log, I picked up a forty-five-pound dumbbell and began doing arm curls to make my biceps grow bigger. An hour later, I'd just about finished going through a mass and muscle-building routine targeting my chest, biceps and triceps when my cell phone rang.

"Yo, this is Mike. Spit it out," I greeted the caller.

"Mike. It's Marlon."

"What's up, man?" I asked surprised that he'd given me a call.

"What are doing tonight?" he asked.

"Nothing. I'm just chilling."

"Do you think you can get out for a little quick party with the football team?" he asked.

"Yeah. I can get out. Where's the party at?" I asked.

"We're headed over to the Tricked Out Night Club," Marlon said. "We have a lot of people coming. It's going to be all that. Girls will be coming in by the carloads. People have been on the phone telling everybody to come hang out," Marlon boasted.

"Now that's the type of party I need to be at," I said.

"I thought so. I know that you're still a freshy—"

"Hey. I'm about to be a sophomore," I cut him off. I wasn't about to start taking crap off of Marlon, especially after getting my photo in the newspaper.

"Whatever, man," Marlon explained. "I know that you can't drive yet."

"I know how to drive," I said not wanting him to think that I was some baby.

"Will you calm down? Dang. I'm trying to tell you that I'm rolling in my father's Navigator SUV. I can come scoop you up in about thirty minutes. Will you be ready?" he asked.

"Yeah. I'll be ready," I said with a large smile on my face.

"Cool. I'll see you in a little while," Marlon said before ending the phone call. I raced through my last set of reps and then rushed back inside to get dressed. I briefly thought about calling my parents to let them know that I'd be hanging out with some friends but knew that they were too busy worrying about Keysha and her issues. Besides, I didn't think they'd have a problem with me hanging out with the guys to celebrate our victory.

Just like he'd promised. Marlon pulled up in my driveway a short while later in a black Lincoln Navigator vehicle. There were three other girls in the car with him. I opened one of the rear doors, got myself situated in the center seat then introduced myself to everyone.

"I'm Francis," said the girl on my right side.

"I'm Ann," said the girl on my left side.

"And I'm Leena, Marlon's girlfriend," said the one sitting up front next to Marlon.

"Nice to meet you guys," I said. Each one of the girls was a ten in my book and I would have walked proudly around the school if I had the pleasure of calling any one of them my girl. I'd seen them around campus before but never had a reason to speak to them. I learned that they were all upperclassmen. Ann was a senior and Francis was a junior and neither one of them showed any interest in dating someone as young as me. I placed my arms around the shoulders of both girls in an effort to appear as if they both belonged to me.

"Boy, if you don't get your arm from around my shoulder, I will snap it off like a twig," Ann threatened me. I laughed a little as I pretended that the bitterness of her words didn't sting. "Are you old enough to drive yet?" asked Ann.

"No. But I'll be getting my permit next semester," I said proudly as I removed my arm from around her shoulder. I allowed my eyes a glance downward toward my lap because I wanted to get a better look at the short skirt Ann was wearing. She must have sensed my eyes dancing all over her because she crossed her legs indicating that her goodies were on lockdown.

"Oh, no, I need a man with a car," said Francis. She and the other girls laughed. "But you are cute. If you were a few years older, I'd give you a little play but I'm about to graduate in the spring and head off to college. You'd be perfect for my little sister when she's old enough to date. She's in eighth grade now."

"Oh, I'm so not interested in some immature eighth-grade girl," I quickly said, insulted.

"Well, she's going to blossom eventually," said Francis.

"I'll bet that by the time you're a senior and she's a junior you'll feel differently."

"I need a woman now. I don't want to wait another two years before I see some action," I said aloud. I didn't intend for everyone to hear was I what thinking. My response just flew out of my mouth before I had a chance to catch it.

"Take it easy, Mike. It's not that serious, man. Francis was just trying to help you out," said Marlon as he glanced at me through the rearview mirror.

"I'm cool, man. I'm just trying to figure out women and what it takes to get a girl interested in a guy like me," I said, wanting to give the impression that my ego hadn't been bruised.

"They'll be plenty of girls out tonight. I'm sure you'll hook up with someone. Especially if you hang with me. I'll show you the ropes," Marlon boasted.

"Marlon, you're not that much older than me. What makes you such an expert on women at the age of seventeen?" I asked. The girls in the car giggled at my question.

"Boy, I don't believe you just asked me that question." Marlon glared at me through the rearview mirror.

"Well for starters," said Leena—who had a smile that would make any guy open up his wallet and give her whatever she asked for. Marlon most certainly had great taste in women. "A young player needs to get a car and some money. You can't expect a girl to take you seriously if you're rolling over to her house on a dirt bike."

"But my sister is dating a guy who doesn't drive," I said as I thought about Wesley and Keysha's relationship.

"Is dude old enough to drive?" Marlon asked.

"Yeah, he's a junior," I answered.

"Well then, your sister is a good one because I can't deal with a guy who doesn't have a set of wheels. I just refuse to be taken on a date via the bus," said Leena.

"I know that's right!" Francis said and twisted her lips in a pout.

"You have to be a well-groomed guy," said Marlon as he made a right turn onto 147th Street. "You can't have dirt under your fingernails, a pile of earwax in your ears or musty smells choking the air from your feet or armpits."

"Oh, God, yes, Marlon. Please school a young brother. There is nothing worse than meeting a cute guy who has body funk!" Ann shouted.

"I don't smell," I said taking offense to being accused of having bad body odor.

"Stop being so sensitive, we're not talking about you personally. We're just talking in general," said Marlon his eyes on the road. "Listen and learn."

"Okay. I'm all ears," I said.

"A girl likes to know that you're into her," Marlon continued. "She likes to know that you're thinking about her."

"And listen to her and the things that she's going through. And don't try to be her hero all the time. Sometimes a girl just wants you to listen," said Ann.

"This sounds like a lot of work," I said jokingly.

"It is, because girls are complicated. You have to remember that what one girl likes, another one will not," said Leena, who gently stroked the back of Marlon's head. "And be loyal to her. Don't go around trying to hump every girl who has two legs, a hole and a heartbeat." I laughed at Leena's last comment.

We pulled into the parking lot of the Tricked Out Night Club for Teens. We all piled out of the SUV, then walked over and stood in a long line of patrons waiting to get in. Once inside we made our way down a corridor toward the seating area. As I walked along with my new friends, I snapped my fingers to the beat of T-Pain. The club was packed. There were people on the dance floor, others riding the mechanical bull and still others just hanging around the perimeter of the club talking. I heard a chorus of voices call out Marlon's name. When I looked in the direction of the voices I saw a bunch of guys from the team holding down some seats for us. I was happy to be among my teammates who all greeted me with an equal amount of excitement. The DJ even interrupted the music and acknowledged the Thornwood High School's State Champion Football Team was in the house.

"What's up, boy?" asked Romeo, our punt returner who'd gotten injured at the state championship game.

"What are you doing here?" I asked. "I thought you'd still be in the hospital."

"They just wrapped up my wrist, gave me some pain pills and told me to come back in a few weeks."

"Cool. I'm glad that you're okay," I said, genuinely happy that his injury wasn't too serious.

"I'm good," he said. "I heard about that touchdown you ran. I heard that you were running like you stole something," Romeo laughed.

"I was just showing people what I could do."

"Well, don't get too comfortable in that position because I'll be back on the job next year," Romeo warned lightly.

"Did you guys hear about the pep assembly the school is having in our honor?" asked Marlon.

"No," I heard Romeo say.

"They want everyone to wear their football jerseys to school. So when you get home tonight, make sure you wash it if you haven't already," Marlon said as his girlfriend came up and looped her arm around him. She pulled him away to a small sofa near a darker section of the nightclub. She sat on his lap and then began kissing him all over. I searched around for Ann and Francis but they'd hooked up with some other dudes and were out on the dance floor.

At that moment two girls who I'd never seen before walked by me and looked me up and down. I knew they were feeling my style. I had on Sean John Poplin Plaid Long Sleeve Shirt with a fresh white T-shirt beneath it. I was also wearing John Decon blue jeans along with a brand new pair of Nike Air Jordans. I smiled at them and they giggled.

"So, what's up?" I spoke to them but they didn't stop to talk.

"This sucks," I said to myself because I didn't want to sit around talking sports with my teammates at that moment. I wanted to be hugged up with a fine honey in a dark corner of the room like Marlon. Since that wasn't about to happen at that particular moment, I turned my attention back to my teammates. We shared a bunch of laughs and talked about girls we'd like to get with and ones that we wouldn't be caught dead with. We continued to talk about which girls were putting out and which ones were just big teases.

Just as the conversation was getting good, I felt a tap on my shoulder. When I turned around, I saw Sabrina standing with one of her girlfriends. Sabrina looked hot from her hair all the way down to the short miniskirt she had on which showcased her long mahogany legs. I looked her up and down twice just to make sure she was the same Sabrina I'd known for years. Even though I had just seen her in church, it was hard to believe her transformation.

"Hey, you," she said with a huge smile on her face.

"Sabrina? Wow!" I said admiring her shape and sexiness.

"What. Is something wrong?" she asked self-consciously.

"No," I quickly answered. "Everything is fine. What's up?" I asked trying to play off just how much I was feeling the new her.

"This is my friend, Katina." She introduced her friend who was okay-looking but nothing to really get worked up over. Katina smiled at me and said hello.

"Will you dance with me and Katina?" Sabrina asked.

"Both of y'all?" I pointed to them. "At the same time?" I asked for clarification.

"Yes."

"Yeah," I said trying not to sound too eager or look too goofy.

"Come on then," said Sabrina.

"Yo, guys. I'm going to go dance with these two ladies here." I knew that I'd look like a straight up player walking away with two girls and that was perfectly fine with me. The guys stopped talking and stared at me, trying to figure out how I'd suddenly hooked up with two nice-looking girls. I placed a slick smile on my face as I backed away toward the dance floor. Once Sabrina and Katina found a spot on the dance floor I stood between both of them. I faced Sabrina and began swaying my hips to the groove of the music. She mirrored my lustful movements. I'd spent many hours in my room behind a closed door practicing for just such an occasion. As Sabrina followed my lead, I felt remarkably special and unique. I felt as if I had a certain kind of charm and charisma that women just couldn't resist. Sabrina flashed her amazing smile at me often, which was a clear indication that she was interested in more than just a dance. *Wow! This is my lucky night!* I thought to myself as Sabrina turned her back to me and began working her hips.

"Whew!" I uttered as I watched her movements. "There is enough of me for everyone to enjoy," I said as I turned to face Katina. She had her eyes closed and was dancing. She appeared to be in her own world so I decided to bring her back to Planet Mike so she could focus on me. I reached out and placed my hands on her hips and attempted to pull her close to me. Katina opened her eyes, smirked at me, then grabbed both of my wrists and removed my hands from her hips. She smiled, shook her head disapprovingly and then made a gesture for me to turn around with her index finger.

"Oh, it's like that, huh?" I said a little irritated because I felt as if she was being a tease.

"Yes. It's like that. Focus on Sabrina. Not me." *What a raw deal,* I thought to myself as I turned back around. Sabrina still had her back to me so I reached out and placed my hands on her hips. Sabrina welcomed my touch and even took a step backward moving closer to me. Just as I was about to press my body into hers, the song ended and they both stopped dancing.

"I'm going to sit down now," said Katina.

"Okay. I'll catch up with you in a minute," Sabrina answered.

"Take your time. See you later, Mike," Katina said over her shoulder as she exited the dance floor. The next song that came on was a slow jam.

"Do you want to dance to this song?" I asked.

"That's why I pulled you away from your friends, isn't it?" Sabrina said sarcastically.

I pulled her close to me and we began to sway to music. "So why did you want to dance with me?" I asked.

"Because I wanted to. Is there a crime against that?" Sabrina asked.

"No. There isn't. I just didn't know that you were feeling me like that," I said.

"Well, now you do," Sabrina said as she toyed with my ear. For a brief moment I had to remember if I'd cleaned them out. I certainly didn't want her to end up with a clump of earwax under her fingernail. Then I remembered that I did go digging in my ears with a Q-tip before coming out, so I was good.

"So, do you like what I have on?" asked Sabrina. She twirled around to give me a good view of her purple cropped jacket and fitted skirt.

"Yeah, girl. You look hot. I mean, damn. This must be my lucky night. Why didn't you tell me that you were coming up here?" I asked.

"I wasn't going to come until Katina told me that the football team was going to be here. I knew I'd run into you. I just didn't know if you'd be with some girl."

"What would you have done if you saw me with another girl, beat her down or something?" I joked.

"I am not the type of girl who fights over a boy. If you were with someone, I would have talked to you at another time."

"Oh, I see," I said as I licked my lips. "If I were your man I wouldn't be worth fighting over."

"If you were my husband, I might fight but other than that, no. Would you fight another guy over me if I were your girlfriend?" she asked.

"I would. Especially if some dude was being disrespectful or if I had to protect you from danger," I said.

"You'd really fight over me? That's so sweet." Sabrina toyed with my earlobe. When she pulled that tender move, all the noise of the club and the music seemed to disappear. I gazed into Sabrina's eyes and they were overflowing with anticipation. I pulled her closer to me and brushed my tongue across my lips.

"You have such succulent lips."

"So do you," I answered. She'd given me clearance to share a magic moment with her. I craned my neck down toward her pausing momentarily before closing my eyes and finally kissing her. When our lips met, she placed her soft hands on my cheeks and sent goosebumps over my body.

"Whoa," I said pulling away because the feeling was a little overwhelming. "For a church girl, you certainly know how to get a man worked up. Where did you learn how to kiss like that?" I asked, wanting to know who else she'd been with. I didn't want to discover that she'd been practicing with the school weirdo.

"From reading *Seventeen* magazine. There is all kind of information in it on how to set up the perfect kiss," she said with a flirtatious glint in her eye.

"So, am I a good kisser?" I asked.

"You did good," she said.

"Just good?" I asked. I felt a little odd because I'd never thought about reading a magazine to get tips on how to kiss. I just figured I'd learn as I go. At that moment, it was clear to me that Sabrina was a little more advanced than I was.

"You did fine," she continued to smile at me.

"Why did you want to kiss me?" I asked. I wanted her to tell me flat out what was on her mind. I didn't want to walk around in circles trying to understand what her motives were.

"Duh, because I wanted to. I've liked you for a long time but you never paid attention to me, Mike. Now that I have your attention, I plan on keeping it."

"Well, you'll have all of my attention now," I said.

"Good, because I didn't go through all of this just for you to start ignoring me again at school," she laughed.

"Don't worry. I won't ignore you," I said, hoping to ease her concerns. At that moment another slow song came on and we continued to dance.

I hung out with Sabrina the entire time I was at the club. We danced through a lot of songs but one song in particular stood out in my mind because Sabrina leaned forward, rested her hands on her knees and shook her behind like a pom-pom and I wasn't mad at her. The church girl had some serious booty-shaking skills. As the night continued on, Sabrina and I talked and kissed until our lips were dry. I didn't even realize how much time had gone by until the club started getting empty.

"Oh, snap. It's midnight?" I said glancing down at my watch.

"What, are you going to get in trouble or something?" Sabrina asked.

"Oh, no," I lied. "I'm just amazed at how quickly the time went by. It's closing in a few minutes."

"Time flies when you're having fun," she teased.

"How are you getting home?" I asked.

"Katina's older sister is picking us up."

"Your father doesn't mind you staying out so late on a Sunday night?" I asked as we began walking toward the front door. As we headed out, I saw Marlon, Leena, Ann, Francis and Katina heading in the same direction.

"Are you kidding me? He'd have a major heart attack if he knew that I was here. I set things up so that I could spend the night at Katina's house. Her parents are out of town. Her older sister who's twenty-one wanted to have the house to herself for a few hours so that she could have some privacy with her boyfriend."

"Oh, I see," I said. It was at that moment I reached for my hip to make sure my cell phone was still there. I removed it from the holster to see if I'd gotten any calls and, sure enough, I'd missed about nine calls. All from home.

"Are you sure everything is okay?" She asked with concern. "You look as if something is very wrong."

"No," I said. "I'm good." I tried to speak with confidence but I don't think that I did a good job. Once outside, Katina found her sister who was waiting across the street in her car.

"I'll text you when I get back to Katina's house, okay?" Sabrina said.

"Okay," I said.

"Think about me tonight," she said as she kissed me one more time before turning to walk away.

"All right, love bird, let's go. All that girl did was dance with you and kiss you a few times and your nose is wide open," said Marlon.

"Don't hate. It's not pretty," I said as I walked back to the car with him.

I was nervous during the entire ride home because I didn't know what had jumped off to make my parents call me so much. I didn't dare get on the phone to call while I was riding home with Marlon and the girls because I would've looked like a baby. No sooner than Marlon pulled into my driveway did I tell him to stop the car and let me out. I didn't want him to drive to the rear of the house where my parents would see his car and possibly walk out and embarrass the hell out of me.

"Are you sure?" Marlon asked.

"Yeah, dude. Stop the car and let me out right here. Just back out of the driveway and continue on. I'll see you at school tomorrow," I said.

"Okay. I'll holla at you later. Don't forget to wear your football jersey," he said. I got out of the car and made sure Marlon pulled completely off before walking up the rest of the driveway. As soon as I reached the back of the house, I saw a police car and wondered what in the world Keysha had done now.

seven

KEYSHA
Monday, November 5th

My alarm clock started buzzing at 6:00 a.m. It was Monday and I had to get ready for school. Once I turned the alarm clock off, I just stared at the ceiling because I didn't want to move. I didn't feel like greeting the day or even talking to people. I was in some sort of funky emotional mood that I couldn't explain. Okay, well, maybe I could explain it.

I'll be the first to admit that I'm depressed but I have good reasons to be. Wesley, the love of my life, has moved to a city two-and-a-half hours away from me. The doctor at the emergency room explained to me that I had contact dermatitis most likely caused by soap, shampoo or even the laundry detergent that I've been using. After conducting a CAT scan which enabled the doctors to look at my brain to check for any blood clots, they concluded that the reason that I fainted and the reason my hair is falling out is most likely related to all the stress I have been going through. First with Liz Lloyd, and now my mother.

Liz started off begging me to be her friend when I first came to town. Then when I opened up and trusted her I discovered she really wanted me to be much more than her girlfriend. She invited me out to a party where she secretly drugged me and tried to take advantage of me. I'm thankful that I was able to fight her off because I don't get down like that. After that episode our relationship changed quicker than she could flip the script. I flat out rejected her and she didn't take it well. Next thing I knew that crazy chick planted ecstasy in my locker at school. The school officials and police found it then pulled me out of my classroom and arrested me. Before I knew anything my entire community had turned against me and was accusing me of being a drug lord. I had to go to court to clear my name.

I know it sounds strange, but I was happy to learn that my problems were related to stress and not some unexplainable thing with my brain. The emergency-room doctor suggested that I stop using all skin care products and use a milder laundry detergent. She also recommended that I see a dermatologist the first chance I got. Finally, she suggested that I limit the amount of stress in my life as much as possible. I chuckled when she suggested that one because she had no idea how much drama I had to deal with.

My latest drama is centered around my mother who planned to petition the court to get visitation rights. She had a lot of nerve to come over to the house once again unannounced demanding that she see me. I mean, honestly, when I lived with the woman, she was hardly ever around and now all of a sudden she's fighting her heart out just to see me. Justine was up to something. I could feel it in my bones. I know her all too well and I know that the only thing she is capable of is screwing up the good life that I have with Jordan. The only reason that I could come up with for her wanting to come back into my life is jealousy. She's jealous that things have worked out for me and now she wants to destroy my happiness. Oh, why is my life so messed up? The only thing going right in my life right now is my grades. I'd managed to pull them up and for the first time in years I was managing a solid B average.

I tossed back the bed covers, walked over to the window and then opened the mini blinds. The sunlight was blinding but I wasn't fooled by it because I knew that it was as cold as an ice cube on bare skin outside. I yawned and stretched out my body. I briefly thought about Mike who had gotten into some type of trouble late last night. I remember waking up briefly from my sleep because I heard Barbara chewing him out. But since Mike had been so mean to me lately, I didn't care about his issues so I went right back to sleep.

I picked out an outfit to wear then opened my bedroom door and headed toward the bathroom. Just as I was about to enter, I saw Mike come out of his room. He had on long pajama pants and wasn't wearing a shirt. There were red marks all over his neck and for a moment I thought that he was breaking out in a rash as well but then realized those were passion marks.

"What's that all about?" I pointed to his neck. Then curious, I asked, "And what kind of trouble did you get in?"

"I got into nunya," Mike said sarcastically.

"What in the world is *nunya?*" I asked.

"It means none of your business."

I gave him a nasty look for being so mean. "What has gotten into you lately? Why are you so cranky all of a sudden?" I asked.

"How long are you going to be in the bathroom?" he asked. He refused to answer my question.

"Oh, you're not going to talk to me at all now? Is that it?" I asked.

"I just asked a simple question. How long are you going to be in the bathroom?" he asked once again as he pointed his finger at me and then at the bathroom door.

"Okay. Have it your way. But remember this, a hard head makes for a soft ass." I paused to give him a chance to respond, but he stood solemn. "I won't be long," I said as I stepped inside the bathroom and shut the door.

After I got dressed, I headed downstairs so that I could eat some breakfast before I bundled up and headed off to school. Just as I was about to sit down and eat my cornflakes, Jordan and Barbara entered the kitchen.

Jordan was wearing a navy-blue pin-striped suit with a silver shirt-and-tie combination. Barbara was wearing a chalk-striped pantsuit that had a close-fitting cropped jacket and a cream-colored blouse. They were having a heated discussion about Mike.

"I'm telling you, Mike is pushing his luck with me," Jordan said as he opened up the refrigerator door.

"I agree with you. He is pushing his luck but I feel that he did this in order to get back at us," Barbara added.

"Get back at us! For what?" Jordan asked.

Barbara paused to think about what she wanted to say. "I think he's feeling neglected," she finally said.

"There is no way in hell that Mike should feel neglected on any level. He's got a roof over his head, a closet filled with clothes, a computer, two iPods and an iPhone. The boy doesn't want for anything," Jordan argued.

"Well then he's just going through some growing pains and we'll have to handle him with a firmer hand," Barbara said.

"I know one thing. The next time he pulls a stunt like the one he did yesterday, I'm going to knock him on his butt," Jordan said and headed toward the door with Barbara trailing behind him. The two of them eventually exited the house and walked to the garage. I got up from the table, walked over to a window and watched as they drove off in separate cars.

"Wow," I uttered to myself. "They didn't even say 'Good morning' to me. Whatever Mike did must have really ticked them off for them to completely ignore me." I walked back into the kitchen and ate the rest of my cereal. Then I went into the family room to watch music videos until it was time to head to school. A short while later, Mike finally came down from his room. He entered the kitchen and grabbed a box of cereal from the cupboard. Then he walked into the family room where I was, sat in the leather chair near the television and clawed out a fistful of cornflakes.

"That is gross," I complained. "Why would you do that? Other people around here have to eat, too, you know."

"What?" Mike asked as he shoved more cornflakes in his mouth.

"That's unsanitary, Mike. Have you even washed your hands?" I asked.

"No," he said and grabbed another fistful.

"Okay, you are really tripping," I said as I stood up and headed toward the front door. I'd noticed that it was just about time for me to start walking to school.

"Whatever, Keysha," he said as he chomped on his food.

"Where were you last night?" I asked again as I sat down on one of the steps and began putting on my shoes.

"Out with some friends," he answered.

"How late were you out?" I asked.

"Late," he answered.

Once I had my shoes on, I stood up to face him. I was waiting for him to tell me exactly what time he'd come home.

"Okay, I was out really late. But I certainly didn't expect them to call the police," Mike admitted.

"The police?" I asked completely shocked because I had no idea that they'd gone that far.

"You mean, you didn't know?" he asked, sort of surprised.

"No. I had no idea. When I got home I was so tired that I went to bed early," I said.

"Well, they freaked completely out when they came home and I was gone. They totally overreacted," Mike said and he came toward me to sit on the step and put on his shoes. "They called the police because they thought something major had happened to me. Barbara was almost in hysterics. Her imagination ran wild on her. She thought that I'd been hit by a car or something and was in a hospital. How she came up with that one I'll never know. So she was calling around to area hospitals to see if I'd been admitted."

"Why didn't you leave a note or call to check in?" I asked as I put on my coat and opened the door.

"I don't know. I just didn't. But I didn't think they'd flip out like that," Mike said as he grabbed his coat and followed me out the door.

"So, what did they say when you got home?" I asked as I watched Mike lock the door.

"Well, once the cops left, they both let loose on me. Dad was shouting at me and calling me irresponsible and Mom was backing him up. I felt as if they were double-teaming me. Jordan kept asking me, 'What were you thinking?' Then Mom asked, 'Where have you been all of this time?' and I told her out dancing with some friends like it's against the law to hang out with friends. Then Jordan says, 'You're skating on thin ice, boy' and I was like, 'What? I answered your question.'"

"Wow, Mike. That's just not like you," I said.

"You know, they didn't even ask me if I had a good time. They're so controlling. They want to control every part of my life and I'm not going to let them. I'm a straight-A student. I don't drink, I don't do drugs, I don't have a bunch of babies all over the place and I've never been in trouble with the police. I'm like the perfect son because I've always followed their rules. But the minute I try to do something for me and make my own decision, I'm suddenly treated like the worst kid in the world. Give me a break. It's not like I was out smoking crack cocaine or robbing people. I was just at a dance club with some friends."

"I understand what you're saying, but next time maybe you should leave a note or something," I suggested.

"They didn't leave me a note or even call me when they rushed you off to the emergency room. Hell, they didn't offer to take me with y'all. They just took off," Mike griped.

"It was an emergency, Mike. They were trying to make sure that I was okay. It's not the same." I tried getting him to understand the circumstances a little better.

"That's the problem. I'm so tired of everything always being about you!" Mike snarled at me. His fury surprised me. I didn't anticipate that type of explosive reaction from him.

"It's not always about me. Why would you say that?" I stopped walking alongside him.

"Maybe and maybe not. But I do know this, if you get into another jam, don't look for any more help from me." Mike turned his back to me and continued on.

I stood there on the sidewalk completely perplexed by his cruel attitude toward me. I hadn't done anything to Mike to cause him to have such deep resentment for me. As I continued to walk to school alone and think about what Mike had said, I came to the conclusion that he must be going through some type of male hormonal imbalance. It was the only thing that I could think of that would explain why he was switching from Dr. Jekyll to Mr. Hyde.

Now that all of the drama with Liz Lloyd had been cleared up, it made going to school a little easier and less stressful. I didn't have to worry about people glaring at me in the hallway or making crazy accusations about me. In fact, a number of students came up to me and praised me for my courage to stand up to Liz Lloyd. As much as I wanted to take all of the glory, I told them that Wesley and Mike were the ones who really did all the work. They both were able to prove that Liz was selling drugs and that got her arrested. I learned that many of the students were happy to see Liz disappear for a while because many of them had been victims of her vicious attacks. One girl named Judy—who was considered to be a little strange because she was always pulling her eyelashes out—came up to my locker between classes.

"I've heard that Liz has been placed in some special type of juvenile detention center," Judy explained. I was about to tell her that I didn't care but she wouldn't let me say anything until she said what she had to. "I also heard that she got into trouble with some girls in there and actually got additional time tacked on. Since she got into some trouble, she has to stay locked up until she goes to court," she finally finished. I thanked her for the information but honestly, I couldn't have cared less about what was going on in Liz's life. I was just happy that all of that mess was behind me.

When the dismissal bell rang, I bolted out of my seat and rushed to my locker so I could pick up the books I needed for homework. Once I'd finished packing my backpack, which felt like a ton of bricks, I hurried out of the building and pulled out my cell phone. As I walked between the school buses and across the parking lot, I called Wesley to see how things were going.

"Hey, honey," I greeted Wesley when he answered. "I miss you."

"Hey. I miss you, too. How is it going? How was school?" he asked.

"Good. A few people asked about you. I told them that you were fine and would be back in a few months," I explained.

"I can't wait to come back," said Wesley as he released a big sigh.

"So, what is it like down there? Have you registered for school yet?" I asked.

"No, not yet. My grandmother and I will do that tomorrow. Today was spent unpacking and stuff like that. There is a high school not too far from my grandmother's house."

"Do you think you'll like it there?" I asked.

"Probably not. It's rough around here from what I've seen so far. I walked up to the corner store and some short brawny dude with a hooded black winter coat approached me and asked me who I represented. At first I said, 'What?' Then he said, 'I said, who do you represent? I've never seen you before and I know everybody around here.' The guy started posturing, then lifted up his coat to show me the gun he had on him. I told him that I wasn't into all that and tried to walk away. The dude decides to stand in my way and call over some other guys who were just standing around the store front doing nothing. They surrounded me and then dude asked if I was with Sur 13 or Primera 18 which I guessed were Hispanic gangs in the area. I suppose because of my light skin tone they thought I was Hispanic."

"Oh my God, Wesley! What did you do?" I asked as I felt a cold chill run the length of my spine.

"I told them that I represented God and began humming a church song that my grandmother was playing during the drive down. The only type of music she listens to is church music," Wesley laughed.

"Well, what did those boys do then?" I asked.

"Well, then dude said, 'I'd better not find out you're representing somebody because if I do, I'm going to put you six feet under.' I told him once again that I wasn't into all of that and he backed off me." Wesley let out a sigh. "I'm going to be in for a rough ride living out here, Keysha."

"Don't say that, Wesley. You don't need any more craziness to happen in your life right now," I said, as I approached the corner stoplight.

"Keysha, I'm telling you the people in this neighborhood look really rough and appear as if they've got nothing to lose. My grandmother said that she was glad to have two men in the house because she feared that the young men and boys who hung out on the corner would attempt to break in to her house and attack her because she was an elderly woman."

"Wesley, it doesn't sound as if you're going to be safe," I said, feeling very concerned about Wesley's well-being.

"I'll be okay. I just have to watch my back around here." Wesley released a nervous laugh.

"So, does your grandmother have enough room for you guys?" I asked.

"Oh, she has plenty of room. She lives in one of those old frame houses that's been standing for decades. I'm sleeping in the room that's in the basement. It used to be my dad's old bedroom when he was a teenager. The room smells a little musty and the bed squeaks a lot but it's clean."

"Do you like it? I mean what color is it? Does it have gray concrete walls?" I asked wanting to get a better sense of how my boo was living. I was also thinking about what I could send to him to help brighten up his space.

"Umm, it's just okay. Like I said, the room has an old squeaky mattress. The walls are covered with brown paneling from the 1970s that looks really old and dated. There is gold shag carpet on the floor, an old record player in the corner along with an old floor-model television set that takes forever to come on because it has to warm up. There are also some old albums on a small shelf. Have you ever heard of a group called Kool and the Gang?" Wesley asked.

"No, not really. I may have heard one of their songs before but I can't be sure," I answered.

"I'll have to see if the record player still works and see what an album sounds like. I'm sure the sound quality is nothing like an iPod or mp3 player. Oh, and there is a big walk-in closet that is filled with a ton of old stuff. There is an old bike, some old clothes, and old *Jet* and *Ebony* magazines dating back to 1979."

"Why would your grandmother keep all of that stuff?" I asked.

"I don't know, but this place is like a museum of sorts. Most of this stuff I think belonged to my dad and grandfather."

"Well. It may be kind of interesting to go through some of it," I said.

"Yeah, maybe, but my grandmother is a straight up pack rat." Wesley's comment made me laugh.

"I'm serious. She even has a box filled with old newspapers. Why would anyone keep a box filled with old newspapers?" Wesley asked.

"I don't know, boo, but if we were to ever get married and you started cluttering up the house you and I would have to fight," I said jokingly.

"Trust me. I don't have any problem letting stuff go," he said, laughing along with me. "I remember visiting her when I was very young and thinking that she had an awful lot of stuff. I remember going up into the attic as a little boy and playing with very old toys from my grandmother's childhood. I'd be willing to bet a million dollars that she still has that stuff up there." Wesley and I laughed some more.

"Well, I've made it home now so I'm going to go in and get some homework done. I'll call you back when I'm done, okay?"

"Okay. If I don't answer, just leave a message and I'll call you back," Wesley said before ending our call.

When I walked into the house, I tossed my book bag on the floor in the family room. I went into the kitchen, opened the freezer and grabbed a box of frozen pizza puffs. I placed them on a pan and then slid them into the oven to be heated up. Just as I was about to start working on my homework, I saw Jordan pull into the driveway. I went to open the door from him.

"Hello," I said as I turned to walk up the steps. "You're home early. How was your day?" I asked.

"Well, my day started out great. At the executive meeting this morning we learned that our ratings have jumped and now we're the number-one radio station in the city. The new director of sales told us that advertising sales are up twenty-five percent which means that I'm going to receive a handsome bonus. Everything was going smoothly until I received a phone call from a social worker." He answered as he took a seat on the leather sofa.

"What did the social worker say?" I asked, feeling very nervous and uneasy.

"We're going to have to go to court, Keysha. Your mother is really sneaky. When she came over here the other day to see you, she'd already filed court papers."

"I don't want to see her," I said stating my position.

"I know," Jordan released a loud sigh and then rubbed his eyes. "We'll fight this," he said.

"When is the court date?" I asked as a numb feeling washed over me.

"Next month in December. Right before Christmas," he said.

"So, I'll be spending part of my Christmas vacation in court?" I said feeling the anger toward my mother growing.

"It looks that way, sweetie," said Jordan. "I'll give our attorney a call so that she can start working on this. Where's Mike at?" he asked.

"I don't know. He didn't walk home with me," I said.

"That boy is going to be lucky if he lives to see his fifteenth birthday next month," Jordan said as he got up from his seat and called Mike on his cell phone.

eight

MIKE
Monday, November 5th

I didn't walk directly home after school because I got on one of the school buses with Sabrina to ride home with her. Sabrina lived on the other side of town. I'd have to walk over two miles to get back home, but I didn't care because I wanted to be with her. We sat in a seat at the rear of the school bus. Sabrina's friend Katina got a little twisted out of shape because I was on the bus riding with my girl but I didn't care. I draped my arm over Sabrina's shoulder and began whispering in her ear.

"You know that I like kissing on you, don't you?" I whispered.

She giggled. "I like kissing on you, too," she said before we kissed again.

"So, is your mom or dad home?" I asked, eager to have some real private time with her.

"No," Sabrina smiled at me.

"So what does that mean?" I asked.

"I don't know," Sabrina said. "We just started really liking each other yesterday."

"That's not exactly true. We've liked each other since we were eleven years old." I thought she'd fall for the line.

"Mike, you have not liked me for that long, so stop lying." Sabrina didn't believe me. I needed her to believe me because I was ready to go beyond kissing. So I figured that, if she believed that I've liked her for a longer time, she'd be more comfortable with lowering her guard and going to the next level.

"Yes, I have. I just never said anything because I was shy. You remember how shy I was back then, don't you?" I asked.

"Yeah, you were very shy." She agreed with me and I was happy that I'd scored a point for deception.

"So why don't you let me come in your house for a little while," I said, as I began kissing on her neck.

"I don't know, Mike. You're moving really fast," she said. "Maybe another day, but not today."

I see that I'm going to have to work a little harder to get around her defenses, I thought to myself. "That's cool," I said. "We can take it nice and slow."

"Really? You're not mad at me?" she asked.

"Of course not." I lied again. I was ticked off on the inside because now I'd have to walk all the way back home and be happy with only receiving a few kisses. I thought that my willingness to ride all the way to the other side of town with her would earn me some big points so that I could at least feel her up.

"Did you know that I still remember that your birthday is on December 29th?" she said.

"Wow. I can't believe you remembered," I said, thinking it was nice to know that she'd stored that information in her memory.

"Every year for the past three years I've always thought about you on your special day."

"Well, you know my special day is just around the corner," I said.

"I know. And I want to do something really special for you. Something that you'll never forget," Sabrina spoke softly and then began kissing on me again.

"How special?" I asked as I offered my neck to her once again. She placed soft kisses all over it.

"It will be so special that you'll remember your fifteenth-birthday gift from me for the rest of your life," Sabrina whispered in my ear and nibbled on my earlobe.

"Oh yeah. It sounds as if I'm going to really enjoy my gift," I said succumbing to passion of the moment.

"So tell me something that you like about me," Sabrina said softly.

"I like everything about you," I said as I began rubbing her leg.

"That's a very vague answer, Mike," she said and then stopped me from rubbing her leg. I suddenly felt as if I'd just lost the point I'd worked so hard to gain.

"I like you a lot." I paused in thought as I searched my mind for something good to tell her. "I like you so much that I want you to be my girl. I don't want to see anyone else but you," I said, thinking that was what she wanted to hear.

"Really?" she said.

Bingo, I thought to myself. "Yeah, really. I want you to be my girl. Just you and me. True love forever." I chuckled a little.

"You haven't known me long enough to love me," she said.

"Haven't you ever heard of love at first sight?" I asked.

"Yes," she answered.

"Let me tell you something." I began to speak purposefully in her ear. "When you came up to me yesterday at church I knew the moment I laid eyes on you that I'd seen an angel. I mean, my heart almost stopped beating when I saw you. I knew right then that I wanted to get to know you even better than I did. Then, when you showed up at the nightclub, I said to myself, this has to be fate that brought us together."

"Really?" asked Sabrina.

"Yeah," I answered her.

"I am so glad that you feel that way because I was so nervous about coming out to see you. I mean I would've just died if I'd gone through all that trouble only to find out that you were dating another girl."

"You're my girl."

"I like the sound of that," Sabrina said and then gave

me a hug. "If you keep talking like that, I'm going to do things to you that I know you'll like."

"Ooh," I said, as her words sent passion chills down my spine. I had to shake her words off me a little because I was happy she was thinking about going all the way with me.

"Well, let's get to know each other really well over the next few weeks so that you can give me everything I got coming to me on my birthday," I said.

"And how do you propose that we get to know each other better?" she asked.

"I'm going to come home with you every day. We're going to meet up at the mall on the weekends and spend time shopping, and going to movies and, you know, just hanging out," I said.

"That sounds so nice, Mike," she said as the bus came to a stop. "Oh. Come on. Hurry up, this is my stop. I'll see you later, Katina," she said to her friend sitting across from her. She quickly grabbed her book bag and rushed toward the front of the bus. I trailed closely behind her. Sabrina and I continued down Robin Lane until we reached her house.

"Well, this is it," she said as I walked her to the front door.

I was about to kiss her one more time but she stopped me.

"No. We can't kiss outside like this. The neighbors might see us," she said.

"So? I don't care," I said.

"Mike, I'm not supposed to be dating or have a boyfriend. My dad would have a fit if he knew that I was seeing you. And the last thing I need is for one of my nosy neighbors to say something to him."

"Dang," I said, a bit disappointed.

"Don't worry. I'll make sure that we have plenty of kissing time tomorrow. Now, bundle up so you don't catch a cold. You have a long walk back home," she said.

"I know. Well, let me get going. I'll call you later on tonight. What time are you able to talk for free on your cell phone?" I asked.

"Seven," she said.

"Cool, that's when my calling minutes are free as well." Sabrina blew me a kiss and then entered her house. I turned and walked back down Robin Lane to State Street, then made a left turn and began my long, cold journey back home.

As I walked back home, I began to think how cool it was going to be to turn fifteen. It meant that I could get a driver's permit, take driver's education, eventually get my own car, and more freedom and independence. As I walked I fantasized about the type of car I wanted. A classic Chevy Caprice with some nice rims and a slamming sound system would be nice. Or maybe if I got an old Toyota Celica, I'd call up the people from the *Pimp My Ride* show and let them hook me up. Oh, I can just see it now. A car with some spinner rims, high-tech sound system, some neon lights on the interior with a flat-screen television that lowers down out of the ceiling. Woo, I'd be one fly brother who'd be picking up all the honeys and getting action on a daily basis. I laughed to myself as I thought about all of the possibilities. Then my thinking shifted to what if I got Jordan's classic 1979 Pontiac Trans Am.

"Yeah," I said aloud. "That four hundred–horsepower V8 Engine with black leather interior and T-Top. Man. I'd drag race that bad boy every chance I got. I'd be like one of the guys from that movie *The Fast and The Furious*. I'd have fun outrunning the police." I laughed to myself as I pictured myself speeding away from a police officer. But I knew that hell would freeze over before Jordan allowed me to drive his precious car. He treated that car as if it were his baby.

By the time I arrived home I was surprised to see Jordan's Honda parked in the driveway. He was home much earlier than usual and that concerned me a little because I didn't want any more confrontations. I was grounded for hanging out so late the other night with Marlon and my teammates. Jordan came down on me hard and wanted me home every day immediately after school. But I wasn't about to follow that dumb order. When I entered the house, Jordan started in on me.

"Where have you been, Mike?" he asked.

"What? I just came home from school," I said.

"Don't play with me. School let out over an hour ago and you live less than a block away."

I sighed and rolled my eyes a little as I tried to think of a lie. "I stayed after school to do some extra-credit homework," I said but I could tell he didn't believe me. "Why are you always on my back?"

"I wouldn't be on your back if you weren't acting so strange. What's gotten into you? Is there something going on?"

"Nothing, man," I said and was about to head up to my bedroom.

"My name isn't 'Man.' It's 'Jordan.'" I stopped and stared him in the eye. He must've thought that I was afraid of him, but at that moment I wasn't. Over the course of the football season, I'd put on a lot of muscle and I'd grown slightly taller than him. I was younger, stronger and felt as if I could take on anyone who tried to harm me and that included Jordan.

"You just remember that you are to come directly home from school everyday until further notice." Jordan used his index finger to thud and jab me in my chest. "Remember that you're grounded for that stunt your pulled last night."

"All right, you've made your point," I said as I backed away from him.

"You just remember this. Every move you make and every breath you take—I'm watching you."

"Can I go up to my room now?" I asked.

"Yes," he said, and I quickly turned and sprinted up the stairs. I hated the fact that he was taking out his frustrations on me. I went into my room and shut my door. I sat at my computer and turned it on. I decided I'd watch a few clips from the *Ultimate Fighter* on YouTube. A moment after I entered my room I heard a knock on my door.

"What?" I yelled out.

"Hey, you." It was Keysha.

"What do you want?" I asked, irritated.

"Jordan's in a bad mood." She stepped into my room.

"Yeah. Tell me something I don't know. He's on my back today for no reason at all," I said.

"I think he's crabby because he has to go to court to fight my mom over visitation rights," she said.

"Is that what it is? He's taking out all of the frustrations he has dealing with you on me!" I accused.

"What?" Keysha truly looked stunned.

"You heard me. He's taking out his anger toward your mother on me. And that's not fair! That sucks, Keysha, and I'm tired of it!"

"Mike, it's not like that," Keysha said smoothly. She thought she could make nice, but it wasn't going to work. Not this time.

"Just leave, okay. Get out of my face," I said and turned my back to her.

Keysha didn't say another word. She exited my room and quietly closed the door.

Over the next several weeks, Sabrina and I continued to secretly date each other. The more we hung around each other the more I liked being with her and spending time with her. Before long, Thanksgiving had come to pass and the month of December had arrived. I told Sabrina that the best birthday gift she could give me was to have sex with me so that I could lose my virginity. She said that she'd seriously consider giving me my wish. That made me very anxious for my birthday to arrive.

nine

KEYSHA
Thursday, December 20th

I could hardly believe that Christmas Eve was just four days away. It was so exciting to be in a home with a family that actually celebrated the holiday. When I was still very young my mother took me downtown and told me that we were going to play a game called "down on your luck" and all I had to do was sit on the ground with her and look very sad. I didn't even think twice about it and gladly went downtown with her. We found the perfect spot on North Michigan Avenue and sat. Then she just started talking as loud as she could. She said, "Please help me get some food so that I can feed my baby." She just kept repeating that phrase and I just kept looking sad and the next thing I knew people just started giving her money. Five bucks here and twenty bucks there. It was amazing how many people gave without question. My mother took in close to nine hundred dollars that holiday season. She didn't care that we had to humiliate ourselves, she justified it by saying she worked hard for it. These days I'm so thankful that all of that madness is behind me.

Barbara, Jordan, Mike and I spent a lot of time preparing the house for the holiday. We cleaned it from top to bottom and pulled out all of the Christmas decorations. We put everything up with the exception of the tree which we would be doing later this evening once Grandmother Katie arrived. I hung stockings, the Christmas wreaths and placed poinsettias all around the house. Barbara and I had gone grocery shopping earlier so the freezer was filled with food. I could hardly wait for all the cooking to start so that I could sample everything.

Over the past few weeks, my skin finally cleared up. I pinpointed the soap that caused my breakout. My hair also stopped falling out which was a big relief because it had finally started to grow again. My court date was pushed back until February 12th, my birthday. That sucked because that meant I'd be spending my seventeenth birthday in court. But for now, I wasn't going to worry about that. I was just happy that this Christmas didn't look or feel like the Christmas I had last year. Last year, my mother pulled one of her disappearing acts and I spent the entire holiday at home, alone and hungry. I could've hung out with my crazy girlfriend Toya Taylor at the time, but she had her own issues. I didn't feel like spending all night listening to her complain about her baby daddy and why he hadn't purchased any toys for their baby.

It had snowed a few times and the weatherman was predicting that we'd have a very white Christmas because a massive storm system would drop eight inches of snow on the ground on Christmas Eve.

I'd already done most of my Christmas shopping with money Jordan had given me but I still had to pick something for Mike. It was hard to shop for someone who had everything. I got Jordan a power-tool set and an electric buffer so that he could wax his prized Trans Am car until he rubbed all the paint off of it. I've never seen anyone wash and wax a vehicle that sat in the garage all of the time. He even washed and waxed it during the winter months. I got Barbara some very nice earrings that she'd talked about purchasing on more than one occasion when we were shopping together. I got my beloved Wesley a gift card from iTunes as well as some new shirts.

I got Grandmother Katie tickets to a stage play about the life of jazz singer Billie Holiday which was playing at the Chicago Theatre during the holidays. She actually told me to get the tickets for the both of us because she said that she thought I'd enjoy it. Since I had no clue as to who Billie Holiday was, I did a Google search on her. I learned that she was born in 1915 and was one of America's great jazz singers, but she had a very difficult childhood. At the age of ten she had been raped. By the time she was a teenager, she was emotionally messed up and sent to reform school. Once she got out of reform school, she and her mother moved from Baltimore to New York. While there she was raped again by a neighbor. She ended up working in a brothel as a prostitute and even went to jail. In the 1930s, she started singing in nightclubs for tips just to survive.

I went on to read more about her life and hoped there was some video of her on YouTube. And sure enough there was. I sat and listened to her music and the sadness in her voice and thought to myself, *Wow. I don't have it so bad.* One of my favorite songs by Billie Holiday is called "God Bless the Child." Something about that song just touched my heart in a very strange way.

I was sitting on my bed in my room reading a copy of *Seventeen* magazine. I was reading an article on how to tone and tighten up my abs when I heard a car horn honking. I got up, walked over to my bedroom window and then saw Grandmother Katie had just arrived. I was so excited that I rushed out of my bedroom and down the stairs to greet her at the door. I know that it's silly for a girl who is almost seventeen years old to be excited about seeing her grandmother, but I was. Grandmother Katie had even brought Smokey, her black Labrador retriever, since she planned to say with us through the New Year.

"Hey," I said to her as I walked out of the house and into the cold air without a coat on.

"Hey, Keysha, child if you don't get back inside that house without a coat on, you're going to get sick coming outdoors like that," she lovingly scolded me.

"I'm just happy to see you," I said as I gave her a big hug.

"I'm happy to see you, too. Now get on inside. Let me take Smokey for a quick walk so he can do his business," she said. Once she walked Smokey, I helped her take her bags up to the spare bedroom and helped her to get situated.

"Just look at my ankles. They swell up these days for no reason at all," she complained as she sat on the edge of her bed and removed her shoes. I was about to close the door and talk to her in private but Mike came in.

"Hey, Grandma," he said before coming over to give her a hug.

"My, look at how big you've gotten. It seems as if you've gotten bigger since I saw you a few weeks ago at the state-championship game." I could see the pride she had in her eyes for him.

"I've been working out a lot. I'm going to try to stay in shape. I'm even going to join the track team in February," Mike said.

"Good for you," she said. "How are your grades?"

"You know that I get all As and Bs, Grandma."

"Good. Well, I know what you want. I didn't get a chance to e-mail it so I made a DVD and I put it right here in my pocket so I wouldn't lose it. Here you go." She handed it to him.

"Oh! Is this it? Is this the entire State Championship game that you videotaped?" Mike's voice rose several octaves due to his excitement.

"Yes, it is."

"Oh, you are the best!" Mike said as he gave her a big hug. He then rushed off to his room to watch the DVD.

"He is so full of himself," I said sarcastically.

"He'll outgrow it," said Grandmother Katie. "So. How have things been going for you, young lady?" she asked.

"Drama as usual," I said as I sat beside her and began explaining to her everything that had happened to me regarding my health and the sudden departure of Wesley. She felt sympathy.

Later that evening everyone had gathered in the family room to decorate the Christmas tree. Jordan and Mike had just gotten the tree situated in its stand. Barbara was removing all of the tree decorations from boxes and Grandmother Katie was working on untangling the Christmas lights. I was standing at the stereo and had just put in a Christmas CD that I'd burned on the computer. The voice of Chris Brown suddenly filled the room.

"Ooh, Chris Brown is so fine!" I said as the melody of his voice gave me chills of delight.

"He's not all that," Mike said just to be disagreeable because I knew for a fact that he'd been practicing all of Chris Brown's dance moves.

"Whatever, Mike," I said and tried to ignore him. We spent several hours decorating the tree, listening to Christmas music and talking. Once we were done with decorating the tree, we all sat in the family room and watched the DVD of Mike's football game. I had to admit to myself that Mike was a very good athlete. I also had to admit that being around all of them made me very happy and I didn't want a thing to change.

On Christmas Eve we all gathered around the dinner table as a family. I'd spent the day helping Grandmother Katie and Barbara cook. We had roast beef, corned beef and a turkey. I made the macaroni and cheese while Grandmother Katie made the stuffing and baked pies. It wasn't easy with three women in one kitchen trying to cook at the same time, but we made it work. I'd never seen so much food on the table in my life but I was definitely thankful for it because I know what it feels like to have an empty dinner table during the holidays. Jordan blessed our food and we all ate.

Afterwards I was so stuffed that I felt as if my stomach was going to burst. I helped Barbara put away the food while Mike and Jordan went into the family room to watch some college football game. Grandmother Katie took a seat in the living room to let her food digest, but it only took a few minutes before she closed her eyes and drifted off to sleep. Once I was done helping Barbara, I went up to my room and called Wesley to see how things were going for him.

"Hey, baby."

"Hey," he answered.

"What's going on?" I asked.

"Nothing much, just sitting around chilling. My dad and I are watching the game. We ate not too long ago. What about you?" he asked.

"It's about the same over here," I said but then heard Wesley and his father shouting at the television.

"Why did he throw that pass?" I heard Wesley say.

"Let me let you go. It's obvious that you want to watch the game and not talk to me right now," I said, hoping he'd catch the hint to pay more attention to me.

"Okay. I'll call you back later," said Wesley and hung up the phone.

I couldn't believe it. He actually got off the phone to watch some silly football game. I wanted to be mad at him but I couldn't be because I understood that he was spending time with his dad and there was no way I could ever be mad at him for doing that.

ten

MIKE
Saturday, December 29th

December 29th had finally arrived and when I awoke I was so ready to lose my virginity. That was the only thing on my mind. Sabrina and I had been dating just over a month and I was ready to take our relationship to the next level. We'd been talking about it for weeks and the anticipation was killing me. I wanted to be at her house first thing in the morning but I had to wait until her parents went to work. But that didn't stop me from sending her a text message which she responded to right away.

Sabrina: Happy B-Day. I can't stop thinking about U.

Thank U. What were U thinking?

Sabrina: Just thinking.

R U nervous about today?

Sabrina: A little. U?

Nope. Can't wait 2 C U.

Sabrina: Same here. Did U get protection?

Yup. U know I luv U right?

Sabrina: I hope so.

U don't have 2 hope. I'm telling U.

Sabrina: How do I know U R 4 real?

Cause it's true.

Sabrina: Can I trust U?

U know U can. Y U ask?

Sabrina: Just need 2 B sure. Don't want U 2 go around telling everybody.

U no I will not do that.

Sabrina: My folks R calling me. TTYL.

Sabrina quickly logged off without saying anything more. I became a little nervous because all of a sudden she seemed as if she wasn't so sure about what we'd planned. But since she didn't call off our date, I was still excited about seeing her. I took some time to download a few more sexy songs onto my iPod so that we'd have some good music playing when the time was right. Once I was done, I put my headphones in my ears. I grooved to the music and practiced grinding my hips in anticipation of what was to come later during the day. I was so into the music and my grinding dance moves that I didn't notice that Grandmother Katie had walked in my room. I turned around and saw her looking at me disapprovingly.

"Oh! What are you doing in here?" I asked feeling very exposed and embarrassed.

"No. The question should be, 'What are *you* doing in here?'" she asked.

I laughed a little to try and play it off. Grandmother Katie looked at me suspiciously. "That was nothing. I was just messing around, that's all. What's up?" I asked.

"What are you up to, Mike?" she asked.

"Nothing, Grandma. I was just in here dancing, that's all. What's the big deal?" I asked getting very defensive.

"You just make sure you keep the horse locked up in the barn. You don't want any ponies running around before you're ready to tend to them. You understand where I'm coming from?" she asked.

I had to think about what she meant for a moment but then I caught on. "Oh. Don't worry about that. I'm not really into girls like that," I told a bold-faced lie to my Grandmother.

"Well, you look like you're trying to get into something."

I stopped responding to her because I didn't want to accidentally slip up and let on to what I was planning to do later that morning.

"I came in here to tell you happy birthday," said Grandmother Katie.

"Thank you."

"Come on downstairs when you get a moment. Keysha and I are going to take you out to breakfast this morning."

"Oh. You guys don't have to do that. Just saying happy birthday is cool. Save your money." I hoped she'd take the excuse.

"No. You're coming to breakfast with us. This is not something you can just say no to."

"Oh, come on! Do I really have to?" I complained.

"Do you have a problem spending some time with me, Mike?" she asked. The expression on her face was a very serious one, it was obvious she didn't like my tone of voice.

"It's not that, it's just—" I tried to apologize.

"You want to put your grandmother down for some little girl who has a hot behind."

I was stunned at how Grandmother Katie knew what I was thinking. I guess she really knew that she'd gotten to the root of the matter by the surprised look that formed on my face.

"Boy, let me read you for a minute. You may have put on some muscle and you may have gotten taller, but those aren't the things that make you a man. Mentally, you're not ready for what you want to do. Physically, you may be but being romantic with a girl takes more than just a hard body. Girls can get very complicated, emotional and vindictive if they feel that your only reason for wanting to be with them is to put their legs up on your shoulders. And I know for a fact that that's all you want to do right now. You don't care about pregnancies, sexually transmitted diseases, emotional attachment or long-term commitments. You just want to get the goodies and move on to the next girl, and then the next girl and however many more you think you'll need to bed before you feel like you're a man."

"Grandma." I wanted to stop her. I hated the fact that she knew my intentions so well. Hearing someone tell you the truth about yourself isn't easy to listen to. "I'll go to breakfast with you and Keysha, okay?" I said.

"And you're going to be with us afterward while we run a few errands. I've already told your mother and father that you'll be with us all day today," she said before turning to exit my room.

Oh, what a raw deal! I thought to myself. I love Grandmother Katie but she's going too far. I've spent a lot of my own money over the past few weeks setting everything up for this day. I've spent money taking Sabrina out to the movies and out for pizza. I've stopped hanging around my football friends just so that I could be with her, and I've been walking an extra two miles home in the cold every day for the last few weeks. She can't ruin this day for me! I won't let her! I sent Sabrina a text message telling her that I'd be there and I couldn't wait to see her.

A short while later I came downstairs with nothing but a bad attitude because what I'd planned to do for myself on my special day didn't count anymore. They were trying to control me. I sat down on the sofa in the family room and watched TV. I was watching Mariah Carey videos and the only thing I could think about was touching Sabrina's body especially if she came to the front door wearing nothing but a T-shirt and her panties like she said she would. The more I sat and thought about having to go to breakfast with Grandmother Katie and Keysha, the more aggravated I became.

"What's wrong with you? Why do you have that sour look on your face?" My mother, Barbara, had just entered the room.

"No reason," I uttered.

"Are you sure?" she asked, a little concerned.

"I'm cool," I said as the next video came on.

"Well, happy birthday," she said as she walked over to me and handed me an envelope with a birthday card in it. "You're growing up so quickly," she said as she reached down and kissed me on the forehead.

"Thanks," I said as I opened up the envelope. There were two one-hundred-dollar bills in it.

"Happy birthday, Mike," said my Dad as he came into

the room. “You’re officially fifteen years old today. I remember when I was your age,” he said, and I thought, *Oh God. Not another one of his boring teenage stories.* “My favorite song was ‘Ladies Night’ by Kool and the Gang. I was the coolest homeboy in my neighborhood because I had all of the latest *GQ* fashions. I had a real rep back then. I was the Philip Michael Thomas of our subdivision and my buddy was Don Johnson.”

“Who are they?” I asked.

“What? You don’t know who they are? Oh my God, how could you not know who they are?”

“I don’t know. I’ve never heard of them? Were they a singing group or something?”

“No. They were the stars of a TV show called *Miami Vice*. They revolutionized men’s fashion back in the day.”

“They couldn’t have revolutionized it too much because their fashion didn’t survive.” I said jokingly. “But I have heard of *Miami Vice*. Jamie Foxx was in that movie last summer,” I said.

“That movie didn’t give the show any justice. When you get the chance, YouTube *Miami Vice* and you’ll see what I’m talking about. I’m telling you. When I was your age I was sharp and a stylish dresser.” I rolled my eyes a bit because I knew that my dad was a total nerd. But if he wanted to fool himself I wasn’t going to interrupt his trip down memory lane.

“Anyway, enough about that. This is your day and I hope that you enjoy it,” he said.

“I will,” I said.

My mom and dad eventually left for work. A short while later Grandmother Katie, Keysha and I went to the House of Pancakes for breakfast. I wanted to eat as quickly as possible and get back so that I could rush to Sabrina's house. By 10:30 a.m. I was done with my food and tired of being with Keysha and Grandmother Katie who both seemed to be taking their time eating.

"Did you stop to chew your food?" Keysha asked. "You pretty much inhaled an entire stack of pancakes."

"I'm good. Y'all need to hurry up," I said impatiently.

Grandmother Katie glanced over at me. "I will not be rushed by you, Mike. I'm going to take my sweet old time and enjoy my food."

I wanted to growl at her but I knew better than to do that.

"He's been acting very strange lately," Keysha said to Grandmother Katie.

"Nobody has even said anything to you, Keysha!" I snapped at her.

"Who are you hollering at?" she barked back at me.

"You."

"Both of you stop it before I do. Mike, you're out of order. Get yourself together, young man, before I do." I could tell that Grandmother Katie had just about enough of my attitude but I had enough of hers. At that moment my cell phone began to vibrate.

"I'm going to the bathroom," I said as I got up and walked away. I looked at my cell phone and saw that Sabrina had sent me a text message that read Everyone is gone. Where R U?

"Damn!" I hissed to myself. I wanted to be with her and not stuck at this stupid restaurant with my Grandmother and Keysha. I sent her a text back that said I will be there soon.

"He's just going through a thing right now but he'll get over it," I heard Grandmother Katie say as I returned to the table. I'd decided to take a different approach to get them to hurry up. I decided that I'd sit, be quiet and tune them completely out. I wouldn't engage in any type of conversation except to answer any questions that they asked. So I sat and glared out the window at the traffic passing by. Forty-five minutes later we were finally leaving.

"Can you drop me back off at home? I'm not feeling too good," I said to Grandmother Katie.

She touched my forehead and the side of my neck. "You're fine. There is nothing wrong with you. You're coming with us."

"You can't—" I caught my words before I said something that I'd regret.

"You have something to say, Mike?" Grandmother Katie asked.

"No," I said as I followed them out of the restaurant and toward the car. As soon as I got situated, I received another text message from Sabrina that said I'm waiting. I groaned a little as Grandmother Katie drove off in the direction of the mall. My mind began racing. I needed to get away from them and I didn't care how I did it or what the consequences were. I was desperate and would do anything to be with Sabrina. After passing up several perfectly fine parking spots, Grandmother Katie finally pulled into one. We got out of the car and walked toward the mall, which seemed to be packed with people searching for after-Christmas sales.

"Oh, we're going to have so much fun shopping today," Keysha squealed.

"I know. I'm looking forward to spending time with you guys," Grandmother Katie said with a smile.

"How long are you guys going to be in here?" I asked.

"I don't know," said Keysha. "A few hours, I guess."

"Come on. Mike. Spending an afternoon at the mall with your sister and Grandmother will not kill you," Grandmother Katie joked. "We'll stop at some men's clothing stores while we're in here."

"Look, why don't you go shopping and I'll walk around the mall looking at some stuff?" I offered. "I might even catch a movie while you two do your thing. I really don't feel like standing around watching you change in and out of clothes. You can call me on my cell phone when you want to reach me."

"I don't know, Mike," Grandmother Katie said thoughtfully.

"Oh, let him go," said Keysha. "I'm tired of him and his attitude. He's a big boy. He'll be fine."

"Okay, you make sure that you keep your cell phone on and don't go into that movie theater because they'd make you turn it off," said Grandmother Katie with a kiss on my cheek.

"I will," I said and turned to walk in another direction. If I weren't in such a hurry I would have paused to give Keysha a hug for providing me with an exit. My plan was to rush back home, grab my bike and go over to Sabrina's house as quickly as I could. We'd do what we'd planned on doing and then I'd rush back home, drop off my bike and go back to the mall and meet up with Grandmother Katie and Keysha. I knew that it was a wild plan but I could do it. I had a girl waiting to take me to paradise. I didn't waste any time. As soon as I left the mall, I began running home. By the time I made it to the house, which was a good four miles away from the mall, I got another text from Sabrina that said It's 1:30p.m. My parents will be home soon. R U still coming?

"Yes. I'm on my way," I said aloud as I rushed into the house and up to my room. I opened my closet door and removed a box from the top shelf. I opened it up and stuffed several condoms that I'd placed there into my pocket. I ran back downstairs, out the door and toward the garage to grab my bike. Then it hit me. My time was short and I needed to get there quicker. Something in the back of my mind said *Take the Trans Am*. Perfect. Jordan would never know that I'd driven it and I would get to Sabrina much quicker. I sprinted back into the house and grabbed the keys for the car.

I knew how to drive because from time to time Jordan would take me out on the back roads and let me practice where I wouldn't hit anything. I fired up the motor, which grumbled and growled. The car had an awful lot of horsepower and it felt good to be in control of it. I put the car in gear and slowly drove out of the garage and down the driveway. Once I got to the end of the driveway I had to wait before I merged into traffic. When I saw an opening, I hit the gas pedal a little hard and the car leaped out into traffic. I quickly gained control of it and sped off down the street toward Sabrina's house.

When I arrived at her house, I didn't pull into the driveway because I didn't want her to know that I'd taken my father's car. I parked the car on the street around the corner from her house. I rushed up to her door and rang the bell. It took a moment but Sabrina finally opened the door.

"Hurry up and get inside before a neighbor sees you," she said.

I quickly darted inside. I exhaled once she closed the door. "Finally, I'm here," I said as I tried to catch my breath.

"Hey, baby," Sabrina said as she stepped into my embrace. I was about to kiss her but she backed away from me. "Ew, why are you all sweaty?" she asked.

"Oh. Sorry about that. I was rushing to get over here," I said. Sabrina didn't look happy. "What?" I said defensively. "I'll go wash up real quick. Will that help?"

"Yeah."

"Well, where is your bathroom?" I asked.

"You can use the one that's upstairs. It's mine and no one uses it but me," she said.

I followed Sabrina up to her bathroom with only one

thing on my mind. When we got to the bathroom, I noticed that there was a shower. "We should take a shower together," I said getting very excited about the idea.

"No. I can't risk getting my hair wet." She handed me a towel. "Clean yourself up and then come out," she said.

"Okay," I said as I closed the bathroom door and freshened up. When I came out I called out Sabrina's name.

"I'm in here. In my bedroom."

"Oh yeah," I said aloud as I walked in the direction of her room. She was sitting down on her bed. It was at that moment that I noticed she was fully dressed. She even had on her gym shoes. I hadn't noticed it when I came in because I was just happy to be there.

"What's going on?" I asked.

"Nothing," she said as she threaded her fingers together and rested her hands on her lap.

"Well then, let's get the party started," I said and approached her. I gently guided Sabrina downward so that she was resting on her back. I hovered above her, looked into her eyes, smiled and began kissing her. I expected her to wrap her arms around me and be more welcoming but she didn't. Her arms did not welcome me and her kiss was weak. I ignored her lack of enthusiasm and began to unbutton her shirt. With each button that I unfastened, more skin became exposed and that excited and thrilled me in a way that I just can't explain. I got her shirt off and exposed her bare skin and black bra. The swell of her breasts and the sexiness of her flat tummy made me want to explore every inch of her body.

"Hang on," I said as I stood up and took off my shirt. I glanced down at my own abs and chest and knew that I had to have looked just as tempting to her as she did to me. I kicked off my gym shoes and unbuckled my belt. Just as I was about to hover over her again my cellular phone buzzed. It was Grandmother Katie calling.

"We've got to hurry up," I said as I tried to unfasten her pants. Sabrina stopped me.

"Mike, wait. I'm scared," she said with a quiver in her voice.

"Scared of what?" I asked. I wasn't in the mood to try to get around her defenses.

"I just don't know about this," she said softly, "It's a big step and it just doesn't feel right."

"Give me a minute. Let's get out of these clothes and everything will feel just fine. Come on, let's do this," I said reaching into my pocket for a condom.

"You're not listening to me, Mike. This isn't easy for me. What will you think about me afterward? Will you still like me?" she asked.

"Of course I will still like you," I said as my phone buzzed again.

"What if the condom breaks? I'm not on the pill or anything. What if I get pregnant?" she asked.

"You won't get pregnant, okay? Stop thinking like that and let's just enjoy each other. What's the problem?"

"I just think—" Sabrina paused. "I mean, I like you a lot but I don't think I can do this right now. Let's just wait awhile. Okay?"

"Wait awhile!" I snapped at her. "This is my birthday. You promised me you'd give me this. How could you mess this up for me?"

"Mike, we could just hold each other for a while, can't we? I'll touch you a little bit." She offered something that I didn't want.

"Touch me a little? What the hell is that? I want everything. I want it all!" I yelled at her and she began crying. My phone rang again. I was on edge. I felt like punching a hole in a wall. "I can't believe you're doing this. You're just a big tease!"

"Mike," she said as tears ran down her face. "I'm sorry."

"I thought you were a woman. I thought you were ready for this. I thought—" My blood began to boil the more I thought about how she'd strung me along. "Do you have any idea what I had to go through just to get over here?"

"No." She sat up and began buttoning her shirt.

"I stole my father's car to get here, Sabrina! You can't do this to me!"

"Mike, I didn't ask you to steal you dad's car!" Sabrina yelled back at me. She stood up and I wanted to push her back down but I didn't. I had to catch myself because my anger was taking control and if I didn't stop myself and leave I'd end up taking what I wanted anyway.

"You know what?" I held up my hands in defeat. "Forget it. I'm out of here. Don't ever call me again. I don't want to see you anymore," I said as I put on my shoes and shirt.

"Mike, you said you loved me. How could you just turn your feelings for me off like that?"

Once I had my clothes on I headed downstairs.

"What does this mean, Mike?" She trailed behind me. She was crying, but I didn't care. I opened the front door and sprinted around the corner to the car. I fired it up and smoked the tires as I pulled off. The Trans Am did a fishtail and I almost slammed the rear end of the car into a lamppost. As I drove home, my phone rang yet again.

"Hold on, Grandmother Katie, I'm coming!" I yelled aloud.

I made it back home and put the car back into the garage just the way it was when I took it. Now I had to run four miles as quickly as I could to get back to the mall. I closed the garage and began sprinting down the street. My phone rang several more times during my run back but I didn't want to answer it until I got closer to the mall. I'd already come up with an excuse as to why I didn't answer Grandmother Katie's calls. That excuse was simple. I couldn't get a signal inside the movie theater. I knew that I'd promised to stay out of there, but I was confident I could smooth Grandmother Katie over. I had about two miles to go before I reached the mall. As I ran along the sidewalk, I saw Grandmother Katie and Keysha pass by me in her car.

"Oh, snap!" I shouted out, "They've left the mall." I stopped running, leaned forward and rested my hands on my knees to catch my breath. I screamed out at the top of my voice. Then I pulled out my phone and called Keysha.

"Where are you at?" she yelled at me. "You've got Grandmother Katie going crazy. She's called Jordan and told him that you've run away from her."

"She did what?" I couldn't believe what I was hearing.

"Jordan's home now. He's pulling into the driveway with us."

"I didn't run away from her," I said, my voice loud.

"Well, she believes you did and she's not happy."

"Let me speak to her," I said. I was hoping to find the words I needed to say to smooth this over with her.

"Tell him I don't want to talk to him!" I heard Grandmother Katie yell out.

"Mike. All I have to say is you'd better get home and quick because neither Grandmother Katie nor Jordan are happy with you right now."

"Dang. I'll be there in a few minutes." I said and hung up. I turned around and began walking slowly back home.

When I arrived back at the house, Jordan greeted me at the door. He grabbed me by the shirt just beneath my chin and jerked me inside the house and slammed my back against the wall. His eyes had nothing but fury in them.

"Why did you run away from your grandmother, boy?" he howled at me like a wolf.

"I didn't want to be with them all day walking in and out of female clothing stores. What's the big deal?" I snapped back at my father. After what I'd just gone through with Sabrina I wasn't in the mood to take crap off of anyone.

"This is the second time you've pulled this disappearing stunt! I want some answers from you, boy, and I'd better get them or I'm going to knock your head through this wall."

"I just gave you my answer. Now stop tripping and leave me alone. And let me go." I tried to jerk away from him. When he wouldn't release me I looked Jordan up and down and glared at him almost daring him to try it. Then suddenly he released me.

"Oh. It's like that now," he said as he stepped away from me and took off his suit jacket and removed his necktie. "You want a piece of me, don't you?"

I didn't say anything. I glared with contempt. I was wound up and angry and the last thing I needed was for him to be in my face shouting at me.

"Tell you what. We're going to straighten this crap out right now. You want to hit me so I'm going to let you."

He was right. I did want to hit him. I wanted him to know that I was tougher than I looked and that if he kept pushing me I was going to push back.

"Come on. Free shot. Take it. Hit me right here in the chest." Jordan drummed his chest. "Take your best shot, Mike."

I clinched my fist a few times as I thought about taking him up on his offer.

"Don't think about it, boy. Do it. I'm telling you to. Hit me with your best shot! Come on!" Jordan growled at me but I didn't make a move.

"Do it!" He pushed my shoulder so I felt that I had to defend myself. He was my father but I had to stand up to him. So I curled up my fist and hit him in the chest as hard as I could. I hit him so hard that he had to take a step back. When I saw that, it made me feel good. It made me feel powerful and stronger than my father. Jordan smiled at me.

"Good. Now hold your chest up," he ordered.

"What?" I wasn't sure if I'd heard him right.

"You heard what I said, boy. Hold your chest up. You're not the only one who uses the gym around this house."

"Jordan, don't do this," said Grandmother Katie who seemed to know something that I didn't.

"No. Mom. I got this. It's about time for this to happen. Hold your chest, boy."

Jordan was about to hit me back. I wasn't about to punk out now, so I held it up for him thinking that there was no way on earth he could hit me harder than I'd hit him.

"You ready?"

I responded by holding my chin up and standing tall. Jordan balled up his fist and kissed his knuckles.

"Mike, this is going to hurt me more than it's going to hurt you," he said and then hit me so hard that my back slammed against the wall and my knees buckled and I fell to the floor. I started gasping for air.

"Get up!" he commanded me to stand to my feet.

I continued to gasp for air because I couldn't breathe. I swear I felt as if my chest had caved in.

"Jordan, that's enough," I heard Grandmother Katie say as I tried to get my breath.

Jordan kneeled down and made me look into his eyes. "Now you know who the big dog is in this house. Try this stunt again, Mike, and I will kill you cemetery dead. Do you understand?"

I tried to say yes but I couldn't breathe.

"Now get up on your feet," he said as he helped me up. "Now walk that off." He said as he patted me on my back.

I kept gasping as I tried to get some air into my lungs. I couldn't believe that he'd hit me so hard that he'd literally knocked the wind out of me. I tried to keep the tears of pain back.

"Jordan, you could have killed him," Grandmother Katie came over and helped me to get up the steps. "He's safe and that's what matters the most," she said as she rubbed her soft hands across my chest to soothe away my embarrassment.

eleven

KEYSHA
Tuesday, February 12th

February 12th had arrived and I awoke on my seventeenth birthday with a sour stomach and a massive headache. Today was the day that I had to go to court with Jordan to settle the visitation-rights issue once and for all with my mother, Justine. Simon told us that he and Justine had a baby boy which she'd named Flip, which I thought was a totally stupid name but my mother was never known for her good sense.

I sat upright in my bed and reached for my phone, which was situated on the nightstand next to my bed. I looked at the phone to see if I had any text messages from Wesley. I had one that said Call me later after court. I sat the phone down and thought about Wesley who was having a rough time at his new school in Indianapolis. Yesterday he told me that he'd gotten into a fight on the school bus with the same boy who asked him what gang he belonged to.

"A fight!" I'd said, totally upset that my man got involved in an altercation.

"Yeah, dude from the grocery store and two other guys jumped me because they said that I was sitting in their seat," Wesley had explained. "I told them that I sat there every day and they need to get lost."

"If you sit in the same seat every day, why were they tripping?"

"I don't know. We exchanged some words and things got heated."

"Well, if it was three against one, why didn't you just move, Wesley?" I'd asked.

"Because I would've looked like a punk if I didn't defend myself. And if I had not, the next time they would've approached me about peeing in the wrong urinal. So I held my ground."

"Well, are you hurt?" I asked.

"I'm okay. A little busted up but I'll survive."

"Well, how busted up are you?"

"Just a split lip and a small cut over my left eye. No biggie. One of the dudes is walking around with a black eye and another one has a missing tooth because I kicked him in the mouth."

"How did you do all of that damage to them?" I asked.

"I don't know. They were swinging on me and I was swinging back. The bus driver pulled the bus over and broke us up. Since the other guys started it, they got suspended for seven days. I'm telling you, Keysha, it's wild down here. Even in the classroom, the kids are disrespectful and a lot of the teachers are afraid of the students. They even broke into my science teacher's car, and another teacher got attacked while walking across the parking lot to his car."

"Wesley, I'm worried about you. You've got to come home. When will your house be finished?" I'd asked.

"Soon, I hope. By spring break it should be done."

"How is your dad doing?" I asked to change the subject.

"He's recovering really well. If all goes well, he'll be back working by the time the house is done."

"Well, that's good because I really miss you. It's no fun at school without you."

"Is everyone still treating you well?"

"Oh, yeah. I don't have any issues at all. I catch wind of crazy stories about Liz from time to time."

"Well, I wanted to make sure that I talked to you before your court date in the morning. Just be strong and I'm sure everything will work out fine. Oh, and happy birthday."

"Thank you, love," I'd said warmly, imagining him next to me.

"Call me before you go to bed."

"Okay. I will."

I stood up and stretched out my body. I turned on the television to catch the weather. I learned that it was going to be a cold one. The high for the day was to be ten degrees but, with the wind chill, it would feel like it was fifteen to twenty degrees below zero.

"Dang, it's going to be cold," I said as I made my way to bathroom. Once I got dressed, I headed downstairs. Jordan was already up and sitting in the family room talking to Barbara.

"Am I interrupting anything?" I asked as I entered the room.

"No, we're just talking about being in court," Jordan said.

"Barbara, are you coming?" I asked. I would've really liked for her to be there for moral support.

"No, sweetie, I'm not going to be able to make the hearing. But I will be there in spirit, okay?"

I nodded my head. "I understand," I said.

"Asia Peking, the attorney I hired, will meet us at court," said Jordan. "We should get going so that we're on time."

An hour later Jordan, myself and Asia were sitting in Family Courtroom Six with a ton of other people who were getting their cases heard. Asia felt confident that given my mother's prior history it would be hard for the judge to allow visitation rights unless my mother had completely turned her life around, which I highly doubted she had.

We all sat and waited for our turn and I listened as the judge was hearing other cases. There was a visitation rights case going on that was rather nasty. One case involved a woman in her mid-twenties who had a newborn and had been denying the father the right to see his child. There was another case where a father took his baby from its mother who had been using drugs and the mother had the nerve to tell the court that she was a good mother and provided a good life for her son.

"These people are crazy," I leaned over and whispered to Jordan.

"I know," he said. Finally our case was called. My mother along with her social worker and court-appointed attorney all approached the judge's bench. My mother must've been seated behind me because I didn't even know she'd arrived at court. To my surprise she actually looked good. She'd cleaned herself up and appeared to be making an effort to do better.

"This is a case for visitation rights being brought forth by Ms. Justine Wiley," the judge began the proceeding.

"Yes, Your Honor," said my mother's court-appointed attorney who looked like he'd graduated from law school yesterday. "Ms. Wiley would like visitation rights to her daughter, Keysha Kendall."

"It says here in the record that Ms. Wiley abandoned the young girl and custody was turned over to her father."

"Yes, Your Honor. At the time Ms. Wiley admits that she had a number of problems for which she has gone through therapy. You should have before you documents that state she's completed a rehabilitation program."

"And who are you, Miss?" the judge asked the social worker who was standing next to my mother.

"My name is Ms. Turner and I'm Ms. Wiley's social worker," she answered.

"Are you responsible for helping Ms. Wiley seek treatment for—" The judge paused as he took a moment to review her record. "—drug abuse, prostitution and check fraud?"

"Yes, Your Honor, I am."

"And how has she done?" asked the judge.

"Ms. Wiley has done exceptionally well, Your Honor. She is drug-free, she's working and maintaining an apartment on her own. She's also caring for her infant son and there hasn't been any incidents of abuse or neglect since she's given birth. I feel that she has come a very long way and with continued support, she'll only do better. At this time, I feel that it is only fair that she have her visitation rights restored."

"Ms. Wiley," the judge was speaking directly to my mother now. "Why do you feel you should get visitation rights after all you've done?"

"Your Honor," my mother began nervously. "I love my daughter and I just want to have some type of relationship with her. I know that she's in a good place right now and I don't want to mess that up for her. I just want to be in her life in some meaningful way. She has a brother now and I want her to get to know him as well."

"Your Honor, we are requesting that Ms. Wiley have visitation rights at least two times a month. If Ms. Wiley continues to improve, we'd like to move to file for joint custody of the minor until she reaches the age of eighteen," said Justine's court-appointed lawyer. I didn't like him very much. He didn't know me, he hadn't talked to me and yet he was trying to change my entire life. The public defenders office probably gave the guy this case just so he could get his feet wet. I could tell that he didn't really care about the lives he was impacting.

"Please state your name for the court," the judge nodded his head toward Asia.

"My name is Asia Peking and I am the attorney representing Keysha Kendall. Your Honor, I would move to deny visitation rights to Ms. Wiley because of the circumstances in which she left her daughter. She left her in a filthy apartment with no food. Keysha ended up in a group home for teens at risk until her father was located. Mr. Jordan Kendall didn't even know of Keysha's existence until he was notified by the State Department of Family Services. Since that time he has stepped up by taking Keysha into his home. Keysha now has a stable, loving family and lives in a safe environment. She's doing well in school and has received favorable reports from her teachers who all state that she's improved her grades dramatically. Although Ms. Wiley has made great personal progress in her own life, we don't believe she'll ever be able to match the standard of living that Keysha now enjoys. Your Honor, it would be a mistake to allow visitation rights at this time and disrupt Keysha's way of life. I move to dismiss this case."

"I'm so nervous," I whispered to Jordan, who didn't say a word. I could tell that he was nervous, too but didn't want to show it.

"It'll be okay," he finally said as I looped my arm through his.

The judge wrote down a few notes and then stood up. "I'll be back with my decision in a moment." He then stepped away into his chambers. I sat there and waited. Wondering if and when my mother would turn around and look at me but she never did. Her eyes remained straight forward. A short while later, the judge returned.

"Okay, I'm going to cut to the chase here. The daughter of Jordan and Justine is now seventeen years of age. The young lady is at an age where she should certainly know right from wrong and good from bad. I understand that she's come from some unfavorable circumstances and has been afforded a second chance at a better life.

"However, Ms. Wiley has seemed to turn her life around and is moving forward and making strides toward becoming a functioning member of society. Regardless of the troubles Ms. Wiley has had in the past, at the end of it she is still Keysha's biological mother and up until the age of sixteen was able to care for her.

"I am going to temporarily grant visitation rights for twice a month on Saturdays for three months. At the end of three months, I would like for each of you to report back to this court with an update. If Ms. Wiley gets into any trouble, has a relapse or places the child in harm or danger before the end of three months, she will permanently lose visitation until Keysha comes of age. This decision takes effect immediately with the first visit being this coming Saturday at the home of Ms. Wiley." The judge slammed down his gavel and I felt as if I'd just stepped on a land mine and was blown into a million little pieces.

As soon as I got home I rushed upstairs and went into the bathroom. I stood in front of the mirror and looked at my reflection for a long moment.

"Why is this happening?" I asked, knowing full well that I wouldn't get an answer. I was feeling a little warm so I turned on the faucet and grabbed a face towel from the cupboard behind me.

"Okay, Keysha," I said as I wet the towel and began the process of cooling my skin. "How are you going to deal with this?" I placed my towel on the towel bar then sat down on the edge of the bathtub, closed my eyes and began to think. The only thing my mind could focus on was speaking to Wesley. He was truly an amazing boyfriend because he really listened to me. I fought myself for a long moment because I knew that he was dealing with a lot already and I truly didn't want to add to his burdens. After going around in circles about whether or not to call him, I finally made the decision to do so. I removed my phone from its holster and called Wesley. When he picked up the phone he seemed happy to hear my voice. After we exchanged a few pleasantries I explained to him everything that happened in court.

"You're kidding me!" Wesley said.

"I wish I were," I responded as I closed my bedroom door and positioned myself on my bed.

"Well, did you even get a chance to tell your side of the story?" he asked.

"Yeah, but they didn't give me much time. It all happened so fast. The judge heard both sides of the story and then went to his chambers. When he returned, he'd made a decision that has changed my life. I mean, how stupid could the guy be?" I asked, searching for answers.

"He has to be completely stupid if you ask me," Wesley said. "Well, what about an appeal? Can you guys appeal the decision?" Wesley asked.

"My dad and Asia were discussing what other options were available but I tuned out the conversation when they were standing in the hallway outside of the courtroom. I just feel so numb, Wesley. I mean, this entire situation just feels so wrong."

"Wow," he said, as the reality of the decision cast a dark cloud over our conversation. "Well, hopefully they can get this decision reversed. Or what if your dad just doesn't take you over there? What could they do?" he asked.

"My dad thought of that, but Asia advised him against not complying with the court ruling. That would lead to more trouble," I explained

"This really sucks," Wesley said.

"I know," I said, then remained quiet for a long moment.

"So in two days you have to go back to your old neighborhood and hang out with your mother all day. I mean, what teenager wants to do that?"

"A weird one," I answered. "I know what's going to happen. We're going to end up fighting and I'm going to want to go home and won't be able to. That's like being in prison without being behind bars."

"Yeah, it is. Man. I wish there was something I could do." He sounded so sad.

"You're listening and that's good enough for right now. I'll keep you posted as to how things are going, okay?"

"Okay. You make sure that you're careful and don't let your mom drive you crazy." Wesley laughed a little.

"You worry about taking care of yourself and staying out of trouble with the gangs," I said to him. We chatted a little longer and then finally gave each other kisses over the phone before saying good-night.

When Saturday morning rolled around, everyone piled in to the car and we drove back to my old neighborhood. The moment we turned onto my old street and I saw the old building I used to live in, chills ran down my spine.

"Oh, we cannot leave her in this neighborhood, Jordan," Barbara said. I could hear the uneasiness in her voice.

"What choice do we have right now?"

"Keysha," Barbara turned around in her seat and looked at me. "If you don't want to go in there just say the word and we'll keep on going." I thought about it for a long moment but then decided it was probably best if I stayed. Barbara didn't know my mother the way I did. She'd have a fit if I didn't show up and cause the entire family grief over a little of nothing.

"If she does anything—and I do mean *anything* that puts you in harm's way—you let us know," said Jordan as he parked the car.

"This neighborhood doesn't look so bad," said Mike who'd never been in the hood his entire life.

"It's cold outside, Mike. In the summertime, a lot of stuff happens. You could be sitting on the porch minding your own business and some fool will roll by in a car and start shooting for no reason at all. It happens all of the time," I said. He was so naive.

"Stuff like that doesn't really happen."

"Don't you ever watch the news?"

Mike opened his mouth to deny my claim once again but then thought before he spoke.

"Thought so," I said to him just to drive my point home.

We all got out of the car and walked up to the building. Jordan searched the names on the slips next to the doorbells to find out which one to ring.

"You'll never find it that way," I said. "The names are probably all wrong." I stepped up to the doorbells and pressed all of them and waited for someone to answer.

"Yeah," I heard the voice of a man.

"Is Justine there?" I asked.

"Naw. Wrong doorbell. Try the last one from the bottom," he said.

"Who is it?" the voice of a woman asked.

"Justine?" I asked.

"No. Her's is the last doorbell from the bottom. It might not be working," said the woman.

"This is ridiculous," said Barbara who'd grown very impatient with this entire process.

"I know, but that's just the way it is," I said.

"What the hell are you ringing my door bell for?" the angry voice of a woman shouted at us. I recognized the voice right away. It was Toya, my old girlfriend who tried to cut me with a razor the last time I saw her. I didn't say anything. I just rang the one that everyone said belonged to Justine. There was silence so I rang it again. Still no one answered.

"Her doorbell must be broken," said Jordan.

I exhaled loudly with frustration. "Guess we'll have to do this the hard way." I stepped away from the door, looked up at the tall building and yelled out my mother's name as loudly as I could. "Justine!" I shouted out.

A moment later a window opened up and Justine stuck her head out. "Hey, Keysha," she said with a smile.

"We're here."

"Okay. I'll be right down." Justine closed the window and I walked back up the steps to where everyone was standing.

Barbara mumbled under her breath; she was without a doubt irritated beyond words. A moment later Justine came downstairs to open the door. She had on a pair of baggy jeans and an oversize blue sweatshirt.

"Oh, I didn't know everybody was coming over to drop you off," Justine said. I had to admit she did look better than she did when I last saw her.

"I can't believe that you slept with her," Barbara uttered

beneath her breath as she gave Jordan a nasty look that said she wanted to knock his head clean off his shoulders.

"Not now, Barbara," Jordan said through gritted teeth. "We fought about this all night long. I was young and stupid when I met her."

"How are y'all doing?" My mother tried to be cordial in a very awkward situation. It was painfully clear that none of us liked her very much. "Nice to see everybody," Justine said with a phony smile. "Well, come on up and get out of the cold. Your cousin Simon is here," Justine said to my father, but no one responded to her announcement.

Once we reached her apartment door we stepped inside. The small apartment hadn't changed at all. The place still felt more like a big square box rather than a studio apartment. On the right wall was an old white stove that looked as if it'd come from the Stone Age. The refrigerator with a chrome handle, next to the stove, was just as ancient. There was a white bassinet sitting in the center of the floor along with a blue diaper bag. Simon was sitting on a sofa near the back of the room holding the baby.

"You all will have to forgive me. I gave the maid the day off," Justine laughed nervously. "I don't live all big and fancy like you guys do. I'm just doing what I can and making it the best way that I know how."

I looked at both Barbara and Jordan who had their noses wrinkled up. For some reason I felt as if their sour looks were directed toward me. I felt the need to say something on my mother's behalf. Don't ask me why. I just did.

"She's trying," I said to them. "She's really trying. I can see that now."

"What's up, man?" Simon said as he stood up to bring the baby over so that everyone could see baby Flip. "I was trying to deny that this was even my baby but you know them blood tests don't lie. Isn't that funny? We're cousins and we both have babies by the same woman," Simon laughed.

"You would be happy over something you should be ashamed of, Simon." Barbara wasn't amused at all. I could tell she was having a difficult time containing her anger.

"It is what it is, Barbara. I wouldn't expect you to understand any of this," said Simon, who was obviously offended.

"You know what, honey? Let's just say what we have to and then come on back to pick up Keysha. I know that she can handle herself but I want Justine to know that if so much as a hair on her head is harmed, I will put her under the jailhouse," Jordan threatened.

"Jordan. There isn't even any place for us to sit down and have a conversation. There's just the one musty-looking sofa over there. This must be that ghetto-fabulous living that I hear so much about," Barbara said snidely.

"We're going to get some new furniture, okay? As soon as I get this job I applied for with UPS. I'm going to buy us some furniture and move into a bigger place. We're going to make it, man. Just watch," said Simon, who was clearly embarrassed by his living situation.

"Look. Mike and I will wait out in the hallway while you guys talk for a minute, okay?" I needed to get out of there. I needed to get away from all of the nasty remarks and ill feelings that were in the room. Mike picked up on my hint and followed me out into the hallway.

"So this is how you were living?" he asked me once we were a few steps away from the door.

"I've lived in worse places," I said. "Sometimes you just have to make the best of it," I said, trying not to let myself fall into a deep depression.

"I'd go crazy if I had to live in a place that small. I didn't even see a bathroom in there. That place is too small for one person, let alone four people."

"So you know that I will not be spending any nights over here anytime soon," I said as a rubbed my fingers through my hair.

"You'd have to sleep standing up if you did." Mike started laughing.

"Keysha? Is that you?" I looked down the hallway and saw Toya heading toward us. She was twirling her shoulder-length hair and chewing gum. She had on a pair of black shorts but no underwear. I could tell by the way her behind was jiggling uncontrollably as she walked toward us. She also had on a black tank top without a bra and a pair of large hoop earrings with matching bracelets. Everything on her was jiggling around and clanking.

"Oh, God. She's the last person I want to see," I said.

"Why? What's up with old girl? She looks hot." Mike seemed to think that Toya's jiggling body was an aphrodisiac.

"You're just on fire if you think that's hot. Toya and I have got a bad history," I said. As Toya approached, I nervously awaited to see if she'd come out of a bag on me.

"Hey, girl," she said and then gave me a hug. I inhaled her low-priced perfume that was so overpowering that it opened up my sinuses. She must've picked up a bottle from the neighborhood Arab-owned store where you can purchase liquor and perfume in one place. "How have you been? And where have you been? I heard you ended up in a homeless shelter." Toya glanced at Mike then back at me to await my answer.

"Yeah. I was in a bad place for a minute but I got out of there. What about you? Did you get Junior back from Family Services?" I asked.

"Yeah, girl, I've been had him back. If the truth were to be told, the family services can take his little bad butt again if they want to." She laughed. I wanted to bring up the fight we'd had the last time we were together but unless Toya brought it up, I saw no need to.

"Do you have a baby yet?" Toya asked me

"No way. I'm not going out like that," I said.

"Let me get this straight. You have a baby?" Mike asked.

"And who is this, Keysha?" Toya looked Mike up and down as if she wanted to eat him alive. "I'm thirsty and you've got this tall drink of water standing next to me. Is this your man, girl?"

"No, he's my brother," I said peeping what Toya was up to.

"Damn, girl. Your brother is fine!" Toya said as she laughed and began to feel on Mike's massive arms. "And solid too. Is everything on you solid?"

"Mike, this is Toya. Toya, this is my brother, Mike. And back off, Toya. He's not for you." I said feeling very territorial. Toya stopped touching on him for the moment.

"What's up with you, girl?" Mike asked Toya. He'd completely ignored what I'd just said to Toya.

"You, baby," Toya giggled. "You got a shorty?"

"I'm not really tied down to anybody," Mike said as he licked his lips.

I thought, *Oh God. I know Mike isn't going to try and mack Toya.*

"Forget about it, Toya. He's only fifteen," I said hoping that would slow her hot behind down. I was also hoping to calm Mike's horny behind down as well.

"Only fifteen? He looks like he's at least eighteen or nineteen," Toya said as she started feeling on Mike's arm again. "You must work out everyday," she said.

"Yeah, I do," Mike said as he flexed his muscle for her. "Because of my size, people seem to think that I'm older than I am."

"If you lived around here, girls and grown women would be fighting over you," Toya teased.

"Is that right?" Mike licked his lips again and grinned hard at Toya. I noticed how his eyes kept falling into the valley of her jiggling breasts. "Then maybe I need to visit your neck of the woods a little more often."

"Maybe you do. Because I'd serve you up and make your toes curl, baby." Toya hadn't known my brother for three whole minutes and already she was offering up a good time.

What a ho, I thought. "Were you heading somewhere?" I asked her.

"Girl, where I was headed to can wait. I was just going to check the mailbox," Toya said as she continued to play with her hair and smile at Mike.

"Mike does not want anything to do with you," I said.

"I think he does," Toya shot back nastily. "You don't know what he wants, Keysha. I think he sees something over here that he likes. Do you see anything that you like, Mike?" Toya asked him as she pushed her breasts toward his face. "Because if you do, you need to let me know what you want and I'll give it to you."

"Oh, I most definitely have to come and hang out in your neck of the woods." Mike got all giddy just because Toya was seducing him. I couldn't believe that he was actually falling for a girl like Toya who is nothing but a snake in the grass.

"So, are you moving back into the building with your mother, Keysha? Toya asked.

"Nah. I'm just here for a visit," I answered.

"Well, damn, girl. Make sure you bring your brother back around. I'm always in the house looking for something to get into or for something to get into me." Toya and Mike laughed at the double meaning of her words. "The next time you come around Mike, I'll put you on my to-do list. You know what I mean?" Toya stuck the tip of her index finger between her lips and sucked on it like a lollipop.

"Where is Junior's daddy at? Are you still messing around with him? And does he still make money by stealing cars?" I asked, hoping Mike would pick up on the fact that she had a man who was a thug. But he didn't because his eyes were transfixed on her wet finger and moist lips.

"Junior's daddy doesn't own me. I'm my own woman. I come and go as I please and do whatever it is that I want. And however he makes his money is his business. Just as long as he takes care of his son's needs, I don't care how he does it."

"Yeah, right. You know that you're still crazy about that boy. I can't imagine you breaking up with him," I said, feeling my old self come back.

"You've been gone awhile, Keysha. Stuff happens and things change." Toya didn't even look at me when she said that. Her eyes were transfixed on Mike.

"So he isn't really around, right?" Mike asked.

"My baby daddy doesn't have a thing to do with whatever you and I decide to get into."

Mike couldn't stop grinning at Toya and it was irritating the hell out of me. *Why wasn't he picking up on my hints?* I was aggravated with both of them. Mike took Toya's hand into his own and began kissing and sucking her already wet finger. My stomach turned at the sight of that. "Oh, that's just nasty," I said.

"Ooh, you're a freak." Toya laughed with delight as she twirled her finger around in his mouth.

"You know, we'll be back over this way next Saturday. You got any plans for next weekend?" Mike asked.

"Only the plans that you and I make," Toya answered.

"So can I get your number or what?" Mike asked as he pulled out his iPhone.

"Damn, honey. You got an iPhone? You must have some money," Toya said excitedly as she leaned closer to him to check his phone out.

"I'm not hurting if that's what you mean," Mike said and waited for Toya to give him her number.

"I'm going to give you the number to my pre-pay phone. So you can't be calling me and talking for a long time unless you give me some money to put some more minutes on it," Toya batted her eyes at Mike and he sucked up the attention that she was giving him.

"I tell you what. I'm going to give you twenty bucks so that you can put some time on that phone because I'm definitely going to be calling you to talk about that to-do list of yours."

"You've got to be kidding me," I said to Mike who then turned to me.

"Why don't you go on back inside and see how your

mom is doing so I can handle my business with Toya," he said and turned back to Toya.

"What? Do you call yourself dismissing me?" I asked.

"Keysha, come on. Just give me a minute of privacy here," Mike pleaded.

"You know what, Mike? I'm going to say this loud and clear so that both of you hear me. Mike, Toya is out of your league."

"Keysha, get out of my face," Mike said.

"Yeah, Keysha," Toya added. "Just chill, girl. I know you didn't expect to bring him around here and not have somebody try to step to your fine ass brother. It's better if I do it than some deranged girl who won't know how to treat a fine man."

"Mike is not all that. He's just a spoiled—"

"Keysha!" Mike stopped me mid-sentence. "Go." He pointed in the direction of my mother's small apartment.

"Fine. Whatever, Mike. Do you," I said and walked back inside the apartment.

twelve

MIKE
Sunday, February 17th

TOYA was the kind of girl who knows exactly what I need, I thought to myself as I entered the workout room Sunday afternoon after church and turned on the radio. I grooved to the music and even did a couple of dance steps real quick because the vibing beat moved me in that way. When I was finished being silly, I went over to one of the blue mats that was situated in a corner of the room and rested on my back. I began doing crunches so that my six-pack abs stayed tight and didn't get flabby.

In between sets I rested and thought about Toya and how delicious she looked to me. She was the type of girl who got right to the point, said what was on her mind, and didn't play around and tease me the way Sabrina had. Yeah, Toya was most certainly a girl that I wanted to kick it with, especially since she already had a baby. The fact that she had a son said to me that she wasn't going to get me all worked up and then chicken out on me.

I hated Sabrina for doing me that way. Although all that madness happened about six weeks ago, my mind still trips out from time to time on how Sabrina played me. But I got her back after what she'd done. When I saw her at school, I made her feel really bad about it. Then I broke up with her, right in the middle of the hallway near her locker, just after dismissal. It was a very public break up but I didn't care because she'd really ticked me off.

"Mike, don't do this, please," she'd pleaded with me when I told her that I was through with her.

"No, Sabrina. I can't do that. Don't call me anymore. Don't come around me anymore and just take my name out of your mouth altogether," I'd said, as maliciously as I could.

"Mike, you told my you loved me, you lying son of a—"

"Aye. If you loved me you would've proven it to me the way I was willing to prove my love to you. So in my book, it wasn't about how much I loved you, it was about how little you loved me. And I can't deal with a girl who isn't totally into me."

"Mike, I am *into* you. Believe me, please," she'd said as she tried to hold my hand. I snatched it away from her.

"Don't even go there, Sabrina! Girl, I loved you so much that I stole my daddy's car to come see you. I faked out my grandmother and almost gave her a heart attack just so that I could come see you and show you how much I loved you. I even tried to beat up my own father!" The words had flowed out of my mouth. "That's how strong my love for you was and you didn't appreciate it. I can't take a chance and let you walk all over my love like that again. I'm tired of trying to get around your defenses to prove my feelings for you. I can't go through all of that mess again. You're too much work and way too complicated for me. So I think it's for the best if we just part ways. Move on. Go find an eighth-grade boy to tease."

"Mike, please don't do this to me. Please don't do this to us. Give me another chance, please. I promise. I'll be better this time." Sabrina started crying. A few people stopped in the hall just to watch our drama unfold. I tried to walk away but Sabrina was holding onto my arm and preventing me from leaving.

"Sabrina. Let me go," I said.

"No. Not until you tell me that I can have a second chance."

"Dang, girl. Let him go. He's not worth going this crazy over," said Belinda who was passing by. Belinda was one of the weird girls in school. She was tall, had a big forehead and looked like a black version of Shrek.

"Listen to Belinda," I'd said. "Even the Shrek knows that you should stop acting like this."

"Go to hell, Mike," Belinda said as she gave me the middle finger before walking away.

"Mike, no!" Sabrina had jerked on me to make me stop walking away from her.

"Dang, Mike. Get your girl under control, man," said Marlon who was walking by laughing at the entire situation. I decided to do what I needed to do in order to calm Sabrina down. I stopped trying to pull away from her.

"Look. Stop crying," I had said and wiped away her tears. I decided to play the role of a gentle, smooth-talking and slick player. "I don't want to see you crying like this."

"Then don't break up with me."

"I just don't see us dating anymore after all that went down. We can still be friends but that's it."

"No. Things can go back to the way they were. All we have to do is just try. I read in *Cosmo Girl* magazine that all couples go through problems. We just have to communicate better so that we can work through them."

"Look. Give me some time okay?" I had said trying to let her down a little easier. I'd gotten her to the point that she felt bad about what I'd gone through and I got her to cry and beg me for forgiveness. I decided not to break her down any more than she already was.

"How much time?" she asked.

"I don't know. I just need some time," I'd said.

"Then I can still call you?" she asked as she began to calm down.

"Yeah, you can still call me," I'd lied.

"Mike, I promise you. I'm going to make all of this up to you somehow," she had said, absolutely convinced of it.

There was no way I could tell her anything different.

I didn't want to string Sabrina along and give her false hope, but in the end, she left me with no choice. If she had a little more self-esteem, my breaking up with her over no sex would not have mattered, at least that's what I'd always been told. But then again I figured her falling apart was just a sign of how strong my game was.

"Okay,"

"Kiss me," she'd said. "Kiss me so that I know you're for real."

I didn't want to kiss her anymore but I knew she wouldn't let this go if I didn't. I kissed Sabrina's trembling lips, which was very weird and then walked her to her school bus. I didn't get on to ride home with her because I just didn't feel like being bothered.

I got up off the mat from doing sit ups and went over to the Smith machine to do squats. It had been weeks since I broke up with Sabrina but, true to her word, she'd been doing everything that she could to get me to come back to her. She kept sending me text messages all of the time. She kept leaving messages for me on my MySpace and Facebook accounts. She even took a picture of herself in nothing but her panties and bra and sent it to me. But I was like, whatever. I had to give it to Sabrina, she was a persistent girl.

After I finished my first set of squats my cell phone rang. I looked at it and saw it was Sabrina calling.

"Dang," I said aloud. "I've been in here thinking about her and now I've thought her up."

I answered the phone to see what she wanted.

"Hey, boo. What are you doing?" she asked.

"Nothing," I answered.

"Do you want to do something later on today? We could go over to Katina's house for a little while. Her parents aren't home."

"No. I have homework to do," I said. I really did have homework but not very much.

"Oh. Okay. Can I ask you a question, Mike?"

"What?"

"You don't have another girl, do you? Because if you do, I'm going to beat her down," Sabrina said with menace.

"You told me that you weren't the type of girl who fought over a man," I reminded her.

"That was then. This is now. Answer the question. Do you have another girl?"

"No."

"Then I'm going to kick Katina's butt. She told me a rumor that you had another girl that went to Thornwood High School and I should just let you go because you were cheating on me."

"How is that cheating on you when we're not even officially together? You know what? Never mind. It's not true. And you need to stop listening to all of those crazy rumors," I scolded her.

"Okay. I promise not to do that. But it's hard not to because you're being so distant with me," Sabrina said. "You don't talk to me as much, and when I kiss you, I feel as if your mind is someplace else. And we hardly see each other anymore. I didn't even see you at church today."

"I got there late. I have a lot on my mind, Sabrina. I'm about to join the track team on Monday. I have to stay in shape, keep up my grades and all of this new drama with my sister, Keysha, has my family kind of messed up right now."

"You know, I'm about sick and tired of Keysha and her drama. I hate how all of her mess has an impact on you," Sabrina's attitude had quickly turned ugly.

"I'll be okay," I said, trying to assure her as well as get her off the phone.

"Well, I have two surprises for you," she said.

"What are they?" I asked.

"Well the first one is kind of bold and I can't believe that I actually did it, but I sent you a photo of my breasts to your phone. I hope you like what you see."

"You did what?" I couldn't believe what she just said.

"I told you. I'm going to get better. I wanted you to see what you have so I sent you a photo," Sabrina said and then was quiet.

"Okay. Cool."

"So, can I get a photo of you?" she asked. I pulled the phone away from my ear and looked at it. *Is she for real?* I thought.

"Yeah, I can work that out," I said, even though at that moment I didn't plan on sending her anything.

"Good. My second surprise is that I've signed up to be the manager of the boys' track team. So I'll get to come to all of your track meets. Isn't that exciting?" she said with enthusiasm.

"You did what?"

"I signed up to be the team manager. I know, it's going to be exciting to be able to see you more often. I'm going to be your biggest fan. I'll be cheering you on every step of the way."

It was at that moment that I began to think that Sabrina might be a closet stalker. "Oh," I said as I tried to think of a way to ask her not to take the job.

"You don't sound very happy, Mike." The happiness fell from Sabrina's voice. "I went through a lot to get that job so that we could be near each other."

I suddenly heard a lot of aggression in her voice. "I'm happy," I lied.

"Good. I'm happy, too. I'll call you later on. I'm going to head over to Katina's house for a little while. Just remember, if you want some of my sweet kisses you know where I'll be."

"Okay," I said and hung up the phone. "That girl is chasing after my pimp juice a little too hard," I said aloud then laughed to myself.

"Pimp juice?" Jordan repeated as he came into the workout room. He'd apparently overheard what I'd said. "What in the world is 'pimp juice'?" he asked.

"Never mind, Dad. It's just a stupid saying." I quickly tried to clear that one up.

"What are you working on today?" he asked.

"Legs," I said.

"Well, I'm going to do a few sets with you. I have to blow off some steam after that crazy meeting with Justine and Simon yesterday," he said. Jordan stretched out to warm up his muscles and then stepped to the Smith Machine and did several squats.

I had to give it to my Dad. Lately, he'd rearranged his schedule to make more time for exercising. He'd lost weight, got rid of the small tummy he had hanging over his belt and, like me, he'd put on a few pounds of muscle.

"So, Mike. Is there a girl that you like at school?"

"Not really," I said, not wanting to have a sex conversation with him.

"Not really? What does that mean?" It was clear that Jordan wasn't going to drop the conversation.

"It just means no. I'm not really dealing with anyone right now," I said as I prepared to do another set of squats.

"Hold on a minute, son." Jordan stopped me. He exhaled a few times and searched his thoughts so that he could say what he needed to. "I want you to take notice of everything that's been going on over the past few months. I know it's a lot, but all of this mess stems from a mistake I made when I was a very young man. When I met Keysha's mom, all I wanted to do was have sex. That was the only thing on my mind at the time. Sex. I made a monumental mistake when I slept with Justine," Jordan said. "I never thought that I'd be at this stage in my life dealing with something I'd done eighteen years ago. My desire clouded my judgment. Lust and desire are very powerful, Mike. Although you don't say anything, I know what you're going through."

"Dad, we don't have to—"

"Mike, listen. That's all I'm asking. Just listen. Lust is a burning, a desire and a strong need to relieve the pressure deep inside you. That pressure will cause you to seek out the first woman who will offer you the opportunity to relieve it. Just because a girl is willing to do you a favor doesn't mean that you should take her up on her offer. I know that it's difficult, Mike. I know that you have a healthy supply of testosterone that you need to get rid of. And I know that at times you feel like you're going to bust open if you don't get a chance to penetrate a girl. As old-fashioned as this may sound, I'd like for you to save yourself for marriage.

"However, I know that I can't be with you every hour of every day and I know that situations are going to come up that you'll want to take full advantage of." Jordan paused for a long moment and bit his bottom lip. I could tell that this was heavy on his mind. "Strap up. Put a raincoat on before you go dipping in some young lady's pond. And whatever you do, make sure that none of your pimp juice spills out. Do you understand where I'm coming from?" he asked.

"Yeah. I understand," I said. I was just surprised that he understood some of the things I'd been going through.

"I know what it's like to wake up in the morning and your solider is standing tall and at attention. He gets up before you, ready for action."

"Oh, we don't need to go there, Dad," I said with a horrified look. Jordan laughed a little.

"Trust me when I say, as you mature, there will be days that your solider will abandon you just when you need him the most." Jordan laughed at his own joke. "Oh, by the way. Your mother was doing some cleaning and found an open box of condoms in your bedroom closet. I told her that I'd come and talk to you about it. So if you have any questions or something you need to get off your chest, I'm letting you know that the door is open, and you and I can talk anytime or anyplace."

"No. I think this pretty much covered it all," I said, feeling rather embarrassed that my mother found the condoms.

"Just a little tip for you. If you kept your room neater, your mother wouldn't be so quick to go and clean it up for you. Okay. Let's finish up our workout," he said as he patted me on my back. "And in case I don't say it enough, I do love you."

After school on Tuesday, I came home and called Toya to see what was up with her. I couldn't stop thinking about her. When she answered the phone, I heard her son crying in the background.

"Hello," she greeted me, but she sounded like she was frustrated.

"What's up with you? This is Mike."

"Oh, hey. How are you doing? I was wondering when you were going call me."

"Oh, really," I answered her.

"Yeah. You've made me wait for three days. I thought Keysha talked you out of calling me or that you just wasn't feeling me the way I was feeling you," she said.

I figured she'd just walked into another room because I heard a door close and I could no longer hear her son crying. "No, she didn't. I've just been busy, that's all. Yesterday was the first day of track practice and when I got home I was tired. But I'm free now so I decided to give you a call."

"So is that how you keep yourself all big and strong? You be doing a lot of running and stuff?"

"Yeah, I do. So why do you like me, Toya?" I asked.

"I don't know. It's just something about you that I like. When I saw you in the hallway, I was like 'damn.' I know Keysha isn't coming back to the old neighborhood with a dude as fine as you are. So I had to come see for myself who you were. Then when I actually met you, I just felt something. I can't explain it."

"I felt something, too when I saw you come down the hall. You had a rhythm to your walk that was like Boom! Boom! Boom!" Toya and I both laughed.

"You so silly," she said, and I liked the way she said it.

"So what do you like doing?" I asked.

She sucked air through her teeth. "I'm into cars. I like fast cars."

"Oh yeah? Like, what type of fast cars to you like?" I asked.

"Well, I like fast toys in general. I like motorcycles. I like the new Dodge Charger, and the new Mitsubishi Eclipse and the Mercedes-Benz SLR McLaren Roadster but that bad boy costs around a half million dollars. I also like classic muscle cars like the GTO, and the Mustang and the Trans Am," she said.

"Oh, so you really know cars, huh?" I asked.

"Yeah, it's kind of like a little hobby of mine," she said, all sweet and innocentlike.

"Well, sitting in my garage is a 1979 Pontiac Trans Am. Completely rebuilt, 400-horse-power engine, T-tops, black leather seats and a slamming sound system."

"Ooh, is it your car?" Toya asked.

"It will be as soon as I get my driver's license. I'm going to be rolling in that car," I said with full confidence.

"Well, are you going to come pick me up in it?" Toya asked. "We could do some things while we're driving down the expressway."

In my mind I imagined Toya doing all sorts of things to me. "Oh yeah, I'm going to pick you up," I said before I even realized it.

"I don't have to wait until you get your license, do I?" Toya asked.

Again before I even realized what I was saying I told her, "Girl. You don't have to wait that long at all. I'm going to surprise you one day and roll over to your house in it."

"Oh, if you do that, you're going to get all kinds of special treatment," Toya said and then puckered her lips together and made a kissing sound.

"I like the sound of that," I said. "So what else do you like to do?" I asked.

"I like going out to restaurants and stuff. Or sometimes I just like sitting at home doing nothing." She sucked her teeth again. "And, uhm, I like getting my hair done. By the way, you should pay for my next visit to the beauty shop."

"What?" I asked because I didn't see a need to pay for her visit to the hair salon.

"Well, you are going to mess my hair up when I see you again this weekend, right? Please don't tell me you're super quick." Toya got quiet as she awaited my answer.

"Woo, girl! You talk a lot of noise," I said, feeling that pressure that Jordan and I were talking about.

"I just want to know because if it's like that, it's not going to work out between us."

"Oh, it's going to work out," I said, feeling very powerful. "I'm going to have you walking around bowlegged."

"See, now that's what I'm talking about," Toya said with a laugh. "I can't wait to see you again because I want to give you some of my sweet tongue." When Toya said that I felt a rush over my body.

"I think I'd like that."

"You're going to like it even more when I see you."

Toya will be the perfect sexual partner for me, I thought. "Where are your parents? I mean, will they be home when I come over this weekend?" I asked even though I had no clue as to how I was going to get down to the city to see Toya.

"Boy, my father is locked up and I haven't seen my mother since I was nine. I live with my grandmother and she goes to church all of the time with my baby. So she doesn't bother me much. I pretty much come and go as I please and do whatever I want. So, when you come over this weekend, you and I will have plenty of time alone. Can you handle being alone with me?"

"Oh yeah."

"Big Mike," she said sweetly.

"Yeah, baby," I said as cool as I could.

"Bring some money so that I can put some more minutes on my phone because you're burning my minutes up," she said playfully, but I knew she was dead serious.

"You got it." When I hung up the phone, the only thing on my mind was hooking up with Toya. My only problem was that I knew that there was no way that my mother or father would allow me to go into the city to see a girl who had a baby and lived down the hall from Keysha's mother. So that meant that I would have to sneak down to the city on Saturday by taking public transportation. I formulated a plan that would work, then I got onto my computer and checked the train and bus schedules. I couldn't wait to see Toya so she could take my virginity and turn me into a man.

thirteen

KEYSHA
Saturday, February 23rd

Having to go through this visitation madness was taking its toll on the family. Neither Jordan nor Barbara wanted to waste time, energy or gas money driving me into my mother's dangerous neighborhood to spend a couple of hours. Barbara, I had to admit, was a real trooper through all of this. I know that it was extremely difficult for her to deal with me moving into her house and welcoming me. Once she and I got past that hurdle, our relationship grew and we learned to like each other. But now, for her to have to turn around and come face-to-face with the woman her husband had a baby with was no picnic.

And my mother, who has a variety of her own issues, didn't make it easy for any of us. Especially with the way she forced herself back into our lives. That was a real sore spot in Jordan and Barbara's marriage. I hear them arguing more than usual and that's not a good thing in my book. I wanted to say something to Barbara but I didn't know how to approach her. I'd decided to call Grandmother Katie and ask for guidance on what I could do to help Jordan and Barbara.

"Let them work through this, Keysha. This is a difficult time for them. They're being tested in a number of ways. But in the end, once this particular storm is over, everyone will have grown and learned a lesson that will make each of you stronger and better people." I listened to Grandmother's Katie's wisdom, followed her advice and decided not to get in the middle of their dispute.

Jordan and Barbara had just dropped me off again at my mother's house and left. I was sitting on the sofa in Justine's one-room apartment looking up at the ceiling because I couldn't stand looking at my mother holding baby Flip who was crying at the top of his voice. Justine began pacing the floor trying to soothe and calm him down.

"Ooh, this boy gets on my last nerve. He's so loud," complained Justine. The more I hung around my mother, the more I began to see that she hadn't changed much. She was still emotionally unstable and it didn't take much for her to lose her temper.

"Do you want to hold your brother for a minute?" she asked as she tried to hand him to me.

"No," I said, looking at her as if she'd lost her mind.

"Well, hold him any damn way!" She yelled at me and

almost dropped the baby in my lap. "Stop acting like your ass has never held a baby before. You see that the baby is on my last damn nerve."

"Where is Simon at?" I asked because now she had me all tensed up and ready to fight.

"He's gone out somewhere. He'll be back in a little while," she said as she walked over to the sink filled with dirty dishwater.

"Do you have any milk for this baby?" I asked, figuring that baby Flip was probably hungry.

"That's what I'm over here trying to get for him. I have to wash out a bottle for him," she said angrily.

"Well, I didn't know," I yelled back at her, which caused baby Flip to wail even louder. "Shh," I said, trying to calm him down on my own. Justine finally prepared a bottle and gave it to me so that I could feed the baby. Once Flip got the bottle he stopped crying. I momentarily studied my brother who was a pretty chocolate-brown baby with silky black hair. He still looked very wrinkly and had puffy eyes but other than that he seemed to be a good baby, especially when he wasn't hollering.

"Thank goodness. That boy was so loud that I couldn't even hear myself think straight." Justine leaned her behind against the countertop.

"Babies are a big responsibility," I said as I made sure Flip was sitting upright as he drank. Justine reached up and pulled down a pack of cigarettes and a lighter from atop the refrigerator and fired up a smoke.

"You know that you shouldn't smoke around a baby," I said.

"I'm not over there in his face. A little smoke isn't going to bother him. Especially with those strong lungs that he has," Justine remarked.

"Why did you even come back for me?" I asked suddenly. "You could've just left me where I was."

Justine blew a long plume of smoke from between her lips. "When I found out where you were and how you were living, I had to come for you. It just doesn't make any sense that you're living better than me and not sharing any of Jordan's wealth."

"Ooh," I swiveled my head from left to right disapprovingly. "You sound just like Grandmother Rubylee," I said.

Justine laughed. Apparently she was pleased with my assessment of her flawed character. "I do, don't I? Simon says that Jordan is loaded. Says that he and your Grandmother Katie have all kinds of money. What do you know about that?" Justine asked.

"What do you mean 'What do I know about it?' I don't know anything," I said.

"Come on, Keysha. You have to have some idea of how rich they are. I know that prissy wife of his comes from money. And I know that big house you're living in with him didn't come cheap. So tell me, how much do you think he has?"

"Why?" I asked. "Why do care?"

"Do I have to spell it out for you, little girl? You know

the type of background you come from. You know what this is about."

I just glared at Justine without saying a word. She looked at me for a long time before finishing her smoke.

"I spoke with your Grandmother Rubylee. She's getting out of prison and wanted to know if it was possible for me to work with you to roll Jordan the same way we did auntie Estelle's husband. We need to do the identity theft thing again. Simon is even in on it. What we need you to do is just give us some information, like a social security number, bank statements and stuff like that. If you do this, we'll make sure that you get some nice stuff," said Justine without any shame.

"Are you kidding me?" I asked, upset that she wanted me to betray Jordan and Barbara. "I'm not going to do that. Not for you or Rubylee. I have a good life with them and I'm not going to ruin it for you."

"Look, little girl!" Justine barked at me. "You have to stop being so damn selfish and help me out here, okay? I'm in a jam."

"I thought you were working. I thought you had a job and was doing better for yourself."

"I did have a job for a little while. I only worked long enough to get access to you so that you could get Jordan and Barbara's information for me. I quit my janitorial job yesterday."

"What? That's crazy. That's insane!" I said as I placed the baby over my shoulder and patted his back softly until he burped.

"Keysha, listen to me. I'm not the type of woman who works at a job. I can't deal with people telling me what to do. I never could. I've always made my own way, did it by any means necessary. I'm a hustler and I'll always be a hustler. Now, if you'll let me show you how this works, I'm telling you, Keysha, you can make a whole lot of money in a very short time."

I felt sick to my stomach when she said that. I placed the baby on the sofa because he'd drifted off to sleep. "You don't have to be this way," I said to her. "You're not trying hard enough to turn your life around," I said, thinking that perhaps I could talk some sense into her.

"What you don't understand is that I want to be this way. I like being this way. Now either you go and get that information for me or I will be forced to file an abuse complaint and get you removed from that big fancy house while an investigation takes place. I know that you don't want to have to come back here to live with me."

I sprung to my feet, "You can't do that!"

"Are you sure about that?" Justine lit up another cigarette. "Remember. I know how to work the system. It didn't take me very long to get you pulled out of that house. Even with all of that money your daddy paid that attorney. They still couldn't stop my hustle." Justine blew another long cord of smoke from between her lips.

I didn't know how to respond to that. The only thing I could think about was being forced out of the house by some elaborate lie that Justine would cook up. "It's not fair," I said.

"I know it isn't. Life is a real funny like that. Just keep this in mind, Keysha. If I'm not happy, I'm going to make sure that you're not happy."

"Why are you so evil, mean, wicked and nasty? Why couldn't you just leave me where I was? I was doing fine without you!" I shouted at her because I was really ticked off that she still had power left to destroy my life.

"Like I said, it didn't make any sense to me for you to be living so good while I'm struggling so hard. Share the damn wealth, Keysha. Because if you don't do it now, by the time your Grandmother Rubylee gets out of jail, she's not going to show any mercy. And by the time she's done working the system and creating havoc for you, that family you're living with won't have a pot to pee in or window to toss it out of. So get your priorities together, girl, because either you're going to help me get it or I'm going to take it. Now, when you come for your next visit, you'd better have some information for me."

fourteen

MIKE
Saturday, February 23rd

when Saturday morning rolled around, I got up early to head off to track practice. I spent all morning doing 200-meter-dash drills because the coach was extremely impressed with my speed and quickness.

"You're going to be our secret weapon this year, Mike," said Coach Miller, who was overjoyed to have such a young, solid sprinter on the squad. I made a few new friends and hooked up with a few old ones from the football team. Both Romeo and Marlon were on the team and they asked me if I wanted to head over to the House of Pancakes for breakfast after practice.

"Sorry guys, I've got something to do today," I said as I was changing my clothes in the locker room.

"Yeah, you're going to go do that crazy stalker girl, Sabrina," said Marlon, which caused Romeo to laugh.

"Yo, I heard that you were in the hallway trying to dump old girl and she got all crazy on you," said Romeo.

"Yeah, I was trying to put her down nice and easy but you know how it is. She's hooked on me. She doesn't know how to let me go. She wants to keep all of my pimp juice for herself," I bragged about how I had Sabrina in an emotional frenzy.

"Well listen up, pimp," said Marlon. "You be careful playing around with that girl's emotions because a chick will turn on you in a New York minute. One minute you think you have your situation under control and the next, boom! She's bringing you all types of drama."

"I know that's right," said Romeo. "I did this one girl and the sex was just horrible. She didn't know how to move or anything so I had to let her go. The minute I tried to drop shorty she went all crazy on me."

"Man, I've told you a thousand times to leave them big girls alone," said Marlon who was clearly clowning Romeo. Everyone in the locker room started laughing.

"Screw you, Marlon. You'd better keep an eye on your girl because I hear that she may have a little something on the side—but you didn't hear it from me." Romeo pointed his finger at himself and continued laughing. Marlon quickly approached him and playfully punched him on the arm

"I was just kidding, man," said Romeo.

"Watch your mouth, knucklehead," Marlon said as he continued to play punch Romeo.

"So, what are you doing this afternoon?" asked Romeo.

"I'm going to be getting busy," I said.

"In your dreams don't count, fool," Romeo teased.

"I wouldn't know anything about that, but apparently you do," I snapped back at him and everyone in the locker burst into laughter again.

"That's a good one," said Romeo, who decided to leave me alone after that. Marlon gave me a ride home from track practice, which was cool because I had a busy day planned and I only had so much time to do what I needed to do. When I got back, I was glad to see that Jordan and Barbara had already taken Keysha to see her mother, which was perfect. I went into the house, changed clothes, grabbed my condoms and took two hundred dollars from my stash of cash in case I stayed a little too late and needed to catch a cab back home. I then headed downstairs and wrote a note that said:

> I've gone out to the mall with some friends. I'll be back later. Call me if you need me.

I stuck the note on the refrigerator so that my parents wouldn't freak out about not knowing where I was. Even though my location was a total lie, it was something that they didn't have to know about.

I walked out to the garage and grabbed my bike and bicycle lock. I hopped on it and rode as fast as I could to the Metra train station so that I could catch the ten o'clock train into the city. After securing my bike, the train arrived a few minutes later. I got on, found a seat and exhaled. It was both unnerving and exciting at the same time to be sneaking around doing what I was about to do. It took forty minutes for the train to arrive at the 55th Street station that was located in Hyde Park, which was Barack Obama's neighborhood. I got off the train and walked down to the 55th Street bus stop. I waited for almost thirty minutes in the bitterly cold air for a bus to come.

When it finally did arrive I felt like I'd turned into a block of ice. I paid my fare, got a transfer and sat down next to a guy with very long, Bob-Marley-like dreadlocks. I took the bus to Dr. Martin Luther King Drive. Then I had to stand and wait for the King Drive bus to arrive. I took the King Drive bus all the way down to 63rd and King Drive and walked back toward Toya's apartment building. As I approached her building, I pulled out my cell phone and called her.

"Hello?" Toya answered the phone. She sounded as if she was sleeping.

"Hey, you," I said as I hurried across an intersection to avoid being hit by oncoming traffic.

"Who is this?" she asked.

"It's me, Mike," I said.

"Oh, hey." She didn't sound very excited and that concerned me.

"Are you okay?" I asked.

"Yeah. I was just out a little late last night."

"Where were you?"

"Taking care of some business."

"Uhm, what type of business?" I asked because I was trying to determine if she'd been with some other guy, which would have made me very upset.

"Baby, don't worry yourself about that. It was just some business. Have you missed me?" she asked.

"Yeah. I've missed you. I've missed you so much that I've come down to see you," I said.

"Really? Are you driving that pretty Trans Am you were talking about?" she asked.

"No. Not this time around. I took the train down," I said.

"Well, where are you now?" she asked.

"Walking up the street toward your building. Can you come and open the door?" I asked.

"Dang, Mike. Why didn't you call me first?" Toya asked.

"I don't know. I didn't think about calling first. I just came because I wanted to see you," I said. "I'm almost at your building. Come down and open the door now," I said.

"Boy, you're lucky that my grandmother has already left with Junior," she said. "I'll be down in a minute."

"Cool," I said and hung up my phone. *This is perfect*, I thought to myself. *It's only 12:30 p.m. so we should have plenty of time*. As promised, Toya came down to open the door. She had on a T-shirt with no bra and a long pair of pajamas with no underwear on. Just looking at her got me all excited. I didn't even care about the scarf tied around her head or the crust that was in the corners of her eyes.

"Where's Keysha at?" she asked.

"In the house with her mother I guess," I said as I trailed behind her watching her behind jiggle around in her pajamas. Toya stopped at Keysha's door and listened for a moment. We both heard Keysha shouting at her mother.

"Yeah, she's in there," said Toya. We then entered Toya's apartment. Toya and her grandmother shared a small two-bedroom apartment. There was a small kitchen on the right side with old appliances similar to the ones that were in Keysha's mom's apartment. To my left was a small dining area that had a small table that was cluttered with mail, newspapers and dirty dishes. Just past the dining area was a narrow hallway that led to the bathroom and two small bedrooms. Directly in front of me was a very small living room with a love seat, two straight-back chairs and an oversize black projection-screen television that took up the majority of the space. Hanging on the wall was a portrait of Dr. Martin Luther King, Jr. and John F. Kennedy.

"Come on back to my bedroom. There is really no place to sit down up here." I followed Toya back to her bedroom which was also very small. Her bed took up most of the space. There were several laundry baskets on the floor filled with clothes, along with several large black trash bags also filled with what appeared to be baby clothes. There was a small closet with a missing door overflowing with Toya's other belongings.

"Come, sit on my bed with me," she said, and I was more than happy to join her.

As I got comfortable in her bed I said, "Oh, it feels so good to be here with you."

Toya positioned herself so that I could rest my head on her lap. She gently stoked my hair and said, "I can't believe you came all the way down here on public transportation. How long did it take you?"

"Two hours or so. But trust me, the trip was well worth it," I said.

"Did you bring the money for my phone?" she asked.

"I don't know. You may have to frisk me to find it," I said as I repositioned myself on the bed and stretched my arms above my head. Toya straddled me and I grabbed her. "Whatever happened to that sweet stuff you were talking about giving me?" I asked.

"I got it," Toya said. I could tell that she hadn't brushed her teeth but at that very moment, I just didn't care. She leaned forward to kiss me. Her lips were full and soft like pillows or clouds floating in the sky. She tugged on my bottom lip and I felt as if I'd died and gone to heaven.

"Damn, you have a lot of money on you!"

I don't even know how Toya got into my pants pocket without me knowing it but she'd located the money I'd brought with me.

"How much do have on you?" she asked.

"About two hundred," I said.

"You were planning to spend two hundred dollars on me?" she asked as if I'd made her the happiest girl in the world.

"Well—"

"Oh, you're so sweet, Mike," she said and hopped off me and out of the bed.

"I'll need some of that to get back home," I said, laughing nervously.

Toya walked over to her cluttered closet and began rambling through it. I sat up in the bed and was in the process of the taking my shirt off when she said, "Oh, no. Keep your clothes on. We are going to the mall."

"What?" I said, completely confused and disappointed.

"Don't be upset. When we get back, we are going to get down. Don't worry about that. We just need to head out to the mall so that I can pick up a few things. You do want me to look nice for you, don't you?"

"Yeah, I guess," I said. But to be honest, at that moment, I just wanted to lose my virginity.

"This will be enough money for me to do a little shopping and get my hair done once you mess it up. Come on. Get up. Get out of the bed," she said pulling me up. "Wait up front while I change and get myself together.

About an hour later, I was reluctantly walking down King Drive toward the 63rd Street El station. It was cold outside and I had my hands stuffed in my pockets to keep them warm. As we moved past dilapidated buildings, vacant lots of land and alleyways, we came across several men who'd set a garbage can on fire. The men were hovering around the fire to keep warm. They all seemed to know Toya and spoke as we passed them by. I got the feeling that Toya and the men had more than a casual relationship.

"You know all of those dudes?" I asked.

"Yeah," Toya said. "They're cool. There is no need to be nervous," she said.

"I'm not nervous. I've just never seen grown men standing around a burning garbage can before. Why don't they just go in the house to say warm?"

"Because they don't want to, honey. Now just relax. I have to stop and talk to these other guys that are approaching us on the street. Don't say anything. Just be quiet and let me talk."

I shifted my focus from the men standing around the garbage can to about six dudes who looked like gang bangers approaching us. I got nervous as hell.

"What's up, Toya?" asked one of the boys who looked as if life wasn't kind to him in anyway at all. My instincts told me that he and all of the dudes he was with had been locked up before.

"Nothing, baby. What's going on?" she asked.

"I just had to straighten out some business around the corner," he said as he looked me up and down. "Who is this Carlton Banks–looking fool?"

I couldn't believe dude called me Carlton Banks from the *Fresh Prince of Bel-Air*. That irritated me and I wanted to say something but I remained silent.

"This is Keysha's brother. You remember Keysha and her mother, Justine, don't you, LeMar?"

"Yeah, I remember Keysha. Simon is messing around

with her mother, right?" LeMar asked, not taking his eyes off me for even an instant.

"Yep."

"Well, when you see Simon, tell him I need to talk to him about something," LeMar said and was about to move on but stopped and got in my face. "I don't like you. You're lucky you're walking with Toya," said LeMar.

"You better get out of my—" I started.

"Come on, Mike. Let that go. We've got plans that we need to keep," said Toya who didn't allow me to finish offering up a threat.

"If dude got something to say, let him say it, Toya. I'll straighten him out right quick," said LeMar as he lifted up his coat and showed the butt of a revolver.

"I'll see you later, LeMar," Toya said and pushed me in the direction of the El station. As I walked along, I began to wonder if coming down to this neighborhood was a good idea. But when Toya placed her hand in mine, and reached up to kiss me on the cheek, I completely forgot about the exchange that had just taken place.

Toya took me to the Evergreen Plaza Shopping Center. We spent the afternoon walking in and out of stores spending the money that I'd brought with me. I really wasn't feeling the shopping spree until Toya took me into a lingerie store.

"Come on. We're going to pick out something that you'd like to see me in when we get back." Never in my life had I ever set foot in a lingerie store. There were all types of sexy underwear for women. See-through stuff, lace stuff, multi-colored thongs and an assortment of other unmentionables.

"This is nothing like the underwear department at Penny's," I said as I followed Toya around.

"No, boo. This is a specialty store. Penny's is for old people. Do you like these?" Toya held up a pair of purple panties.

"They look good to me," I said grinning at her.

"Would you like to see me in these later on today?"

"Yeah," I said.

"What about these?" Toya held up a hot red thong with a matching bra.

"Ooh," was all I could say.

Toya then placed the garment against her waistline. "Do you think these will look good on me?" she asked.

"Yeah. Get both of them," I said because I was eager to make the purchase and get back so that I could see her in them.

Toya purchased the undergarments and several other items and then we left that store and headed to a shoe store and then to the beauty-supply shop before heading back to her place.

By the time we'd gotten back it was dark and almost 5:00 p.m. and I had to get back. I was very disappointed that time had gotten away and that once again I'd gone through a whole lot of effort for nothing.

"Look, Toya. I'm going to head on home," I said as soon as we entered her apartment.

"Now, wait a minute. Don't rush off just yet. You

haven't even seen me try on the lingerie yet. Don't you want to see what it looks like on my skin?" Toya was talking more seductively than she had been before.

"Toya," I said.

"Shh," she placed her index finger up to my lips. "I know you want this," she said as she stepped into my embrace and kissed me. Those soft lips and her seductive eyes put me under a spell. I lightly caressed her back but she grabbed my arms at my wrists and placed them on her derriere, which was just as soft as her lips.

"Now, come on back here into my room so that I can keep my promise." She pulled me along and I followed her. "Take off your clothes," she said. "I'm going to go into the bathroom and freshen up." Toya turned and exited the room.

"Ooh, yes!" I said aloud as I took off my coat, and kicked off my shoes. I was about to unbuckle my pants when I heard her front door open. I paused like a deer caught in headlights. Toya came rushing back into the room. She was still fully dressed.

"Hurry up. Hide in the closest," she said.

"Hide?" I asked, confused.

"Just get in there," she whispered loudly.

"There's too much stuff in there," I said.

"Just step on it! My grandmother is home early and you're not supposed to be here. Her sight is bad but she's not crazy," Toya said as I stuffed myself into her closet. I scooted down as best as I could and she tossed bags of clothes on me.

"Wait here."

"For how long?" I asked, but Toya had walked away and closed her bedroom door. At that moment, my cell phone began to vibrate. I pulled it out and looked at it. Jordan was calling me.

"Damn, damn, damn!" I hissed through gritted teeth. I didn't answer the phone because I was too afraid. I just wanted to get out of the closet and get back home. Thankfully, Toya didn't take long.

"Come on. She's in her bedroom. Get your stuff, get out and call me later." She said as I picked up my belongings. As I walked toward the front door I saw a little boy sitting in a booster seat eating a graham cracker.

"Call me later. I promise you the next time you come over, we're going to get down," Toya said as she pushed me out of the door and into the hallway.

I put on my shoes and coat and rushed out of the building. Just as I was about to exit I saw LeMar the thug and his goons. *Damn*, I thought to myself. I don't want any drama with this dude because he has a gun. I don't want my life to end over something dumb. I cautiously opened the door, swerved around LeMar and his goons who stopped talking and glared at me as I moved past them. Once I was out of their way I began running at top speed to get out of the neighborhood. The only thing on my mind at that point was getting back home as quickly as I could. Once I got on a bus. I called home to check in as well as to let Jordan know that I was on my way.

fifteen

KEYSHA
Thursday, February 28th

I wasn't about to allow my mother to ruin the good life that I had with Jordan, Barbara and Mike. If she thought for one second that I was going to provide her with enough information to rip off my dad she had another thing coming. Justine is such a psychopath and she really needs to seek professional help. My grandmother Rubylee does as well. I just hope that she doesn't try to look me up when she gets out of prison.

Thankfully, my two visits to her for the month of February had come and passed. So I didn't have to worry about another visit with her until March. I had two more visits to go before going back to court for the judge to reevaluate my situation. I was confident that he'd permanently deny visitation rights especially once he found out that she wasn't working. By that time, I was hoping and praying that Wesley would be back so that we could do some serious catching up.

On Thursday when I returned home from school, I noticed that Barbara's car was sitting in the driveway.

"I wonder why she's home early," I said aloud as I walked up the driveway. When I got to the door, Barbara opened it up to let me in.

"Hey," I said as I stepped inside.

"Hello, Keysha. Where is Mike? He isn't with you?" she asked.

"No. I think he had track practice," I said.

"Oh, that's right. I forgot," she said as she shut the door and locked it behind her.

"What are you doing home so early?"

"I just needed a break," Barbara said. "So today I just said 'the heck with it.' I'm going home to relax and take it easy. These last few weeks have been murder."

"I know. Life can really suck sometimes," I said, and I placed my heavy book bag down. "I'm so sorry that you have to go through all of this drama with my mother. She's crazy. I wish it weren't true, but it is," I apologized, feeling a little responsible for the added stress in Barbara's life.

"Honey, don't worry about it. I'm a big girl and I can take a lot. Sometimes things may get me down but I always bounce back," she said with a smile.

"Can I do anything for you?" I asked.

"No," Barbara answered. "Is there anything that I can do for you?"

"No. I'm good. I think I'm going to give myself a footbath though. My feet are killing me."

"You know. I have an even better idea. Why don't we turn on the fireplace, give ourselves a footbath there, eat some ice cream and chat for a while? We haven't had a good chitchat in sometime now. What do you say?" she asked.

"Sounds like a plan to me," I said. "I'll go and get the footbaths," I offered as I headed off.

"And I'll turn on the fireplace."

A short while later Barbara and I were sitting all cozy and warm with our feet submerged in warm water while eating ice cream.

"So, what's it like spending time with your mother?" she asked.

"It's okay, I guess," I said.

"Just okay?" Barbara was prying a little.

"Like I said before, Justine isn't the most stable woman in the world. She's always making things so complicated and difficult when they don't have to be," I confided.

"She's not harming you in any way is she?"

"No, she's not," I said as I took my wet feet out of the footbath and held them up in front of the warm flames. "Ooh, that feels good," I said, laughing a little before placing my feet back in the water. "I'm in a strange emotional place with my mother."

"What do you mean by that?" asked Barbara.

"It's like I'm numb when I'm around her. I don't have any feelings for her. Is that bad?" I asked.

Barbara inhaled and exhaled deeply. "I kind of know what page you're on. When my sister was strung out on drugs, there came a time when my heart grew cold toward her. I'd grown tired of her treacherous ways. I was tired of all her lies and excuses. As a result, I just couldn't allow her to get close to me anymore."

"You never talk about how your sister is doing now. I never hear her call or anything."

"Oh, she's okay. She calls me on my cell phone and we communicate that way," Barbara said.

"How did you get to the point that you learned to like or even trust her again?" I asked.

"Prayer. And a lot of it. When she turned her life around and stuck to her guns, I gained more respect for her because I knew that what she'd gone through wasn't easy. The life choices she made were not easy but she had to recognize that for herself. I along with my parents could've told her that until we were blue in the face. But that was a lesson that my sister had to learn."

"My mother needs to learn some lessons. That's for sure."

"Honey, I think as long as we keep on breathing there will be lessons to be learned. Even at this point in my life, I'm still learning a lot," she confessed. "One thing that I've recently learned is just how strong, beautiful and smart you are. After I saw the apartment that you were living in, I was so amazed that you didn't get caught up in the traps that your mother's lifestyle offered. You have such a strong and smart mind. Don't ever let anyone tell you differently."

"Aw, thank you," I said, feeling the warmth of the compliment.

"Have you thought about college at all, Keysha? Next year, you'll be a senior and I believe you'll be taking the ACT and SAT tests soon. Am I correct?"

"Yes. My counselor, Mr. Sanders, has mentioned it to me several times already," I said. "I haven't given it much thought because college just wasn't in my original life plan. When I was living with my mom, I just knew that I was going to get a job directly after high school and take care of my own immediate needs, like a roof over my head and food in my belly."

"I would imagine that there are a lot of kids out there who are struggling with some of the same issues that you had."

"When I lived in my old neighborhood, practically everyone that I knew had some type of malfunctioning or irresponsible parent."

"That's sad," Barbara said. There was a long moment of silence between us as we listened to the wood in the fireplace crackle. "Do you know what we need right now?" Barbara asked.

"No, what?"

"Some relaxing music." Barbara reached over to a nearby end table and picked up the stereo remote. She aimed it at the audio system and scrolled until she found her favorite smooth jazz station. Singer Jill Scott was singing a rendition of an old Billie Holiday song.

"Grandmother Katie and I went to see a stage play

about her life story back during the holiday," I reminded Barbara.

"I know. She told me that you guys had a wonderful time and that you started crying at the part when Billie got strung out on drugs."

"It was so sad. I'm mean, after all she'd gone through. She was raped, lived in a bad neighborhood and had to turn to prostitution to survive. Talk about heartache," I said.

"Yep. That's why this song touches so many hearts. Everyone is going to know a little heartache at some point in their life," Barbara said as she sang along. The next song that came on was by Sade.

"You know Sade and Billie Holiday have very similar styles. Their voices are very mellowing and soothing," I said.

"Oh, don't I know it. I love me some Sade," Barbara said as she popped her fingers.

"Yeah," I said as I just sat back and enjoyed the mellow moment and peacefulness of being with Barbara.

Sometimes it seems like time is moving quicker than I'd like it to because February ended and the first Saturday in March arrived. I hated being forced to put up with my visits with Justine. I just knew she was going to be on my back about getting the account information she wanted. So I decided to write down a bunch of fake information and try to talk some sense into her before she did something to mess up her life as well my brother Flip's life. I certainly feel sorry for Flip because he's in for a rough time dealing with Justine and Simon.

I came downstairs Saturday morning ready to go visit Justine and get through a day of stress and mental torture.

"Are you ready?" Jordan asked as we prepared to leave.

"Yeah, I'm ready," I said as I stuck an envelope with the bogus account information in my purse.

"Don't worry. Asia is working really hard to do something about these visits. If Justine messes up in any way, we can get the court to overturn this decision."

"It's okay Dad, I can handle myself. Remember, I've lived with Justine all of my life so I know how to deal with her. I'll just be glad when I turn eighteen so that I can start making some of my own decisions and choices," I said.

"Well, you'll turn eighteen soon enough," Jordan said as he walked into the family room and opened up the plantation shutters to let some sunlight come in. "Barbara and I are going to head over to the McCormick Place Convention Center and hang around at the auto show while you're visiting. By late afternoon, we'll be back to pick you up. Okay?"

"Okay," I said. "Is Mike going with you guys?" I asked.

"No. Mike went to his friend Marlon's birthday party yesterday, remember?" said Jordan.

"Oh, yeah. That's right, I forgot all about that. But I'm still surprised that he doesn't want to go to the auto show." I said.

"I know one thing. Mike is starting to hang out a little too much. I'm giving him a little slack but if his grades have fallen off in any way, he's going to have to deal with me." Jordan walked back into the kitchen. "That goes for you, too," he said.

"Trust me when I say that my grades are doing a lot better than they have been for a long time," I said as I moved toward the door to put on my gym shoes.

About forty minutes later I was knocking on Justine's apartment door. When she opened up, she had Flip in one arm while she held a cigarette between the fingers of her other hand.

"Here. Take him," she said as he handed him to me.

"He's all wet," I said as I took him in my arms.

"Change him for me," she said as she walked toward the bathroom.

I lowered my eyes to slits because the last thing I wanted to do was change a dirty diaper. "I don't know how to change a baby," I said.

"Figure it out then," she said as she slammed the bathroom door shut.

"Ooh, you make me sick!" I snapped at her.

"You make me sick, too," she shouted back through the closed door.

I laid Flip down on the sofa and reached into the diaper bag that was nearby. I pulled out some baby wipes, a clean diaper and began changing him. By the time I was done. Justine was exiting the bathroom.

"So, did you get that information for me?" she asked.

I cut my eyes at her.

"Well?" she continued.

"Yeah. I got something for you," I said. I was about to start trying to talk her out of making another dumb mistake but then Simon arrived.

"Hey. I just saw Jordan pull off not too long ago. Did Keysha get what we needed?" he asked.

"How could you do this to your own cousin?" I snapped at him.

"It's better that I do it than a total stranger, don't you think?" It was like he had no sense of right or wrong.

"But this is so mean," I said.

"Well, we couldn't pull this off without your help. So you must be just as mean as we are," he said as he walked over to the sofa to pick up his son, played with him for a moment and then sat him back down like a toy he'd gotten bored with. I looked at them both suspiciously. They were up to something much bigger than what I thought. Simon walked over and invaded my space. He was much too close to me.

"How old are you now, Keysha?" asked Simon.

"Seventeen," I said as I backed away. Simon kept moving forward until my back was up against the refrigerator. Simon looked at my lips and then down at the swell of my breasts. He was molesting me with his eyes.

"You certainly are a feisty little girl," he began breathing heavily.

"Leave her alone, Simon," Justine tried to intervene but Simon didn't listen to her. Simon placed both of his hands against the refrigerator and blocked me in.

"It's going to take a man like me to break you down. We could both make some good money if you'd get out there on foot patrol for me."

I couldn't believe he'd just said that to me. He actually thought that I was going to turn to a life of prostitution for him. I thought for sure Justine would say something, but she didn't. She didn't try to protect me or pull him from in front of my face.

"Get away from me," I said looking him directly in the eyes. I wanted to let him know that I wasn't afraid of him.

"Yeah. I'm going to have a real good time breaking you down," he said as he slammed his fist against the refrigerator. The loud noise startled me.

"Justine, I'll be outside waiting for you in the car. Don't be too long. You know that we're on a tight schedule," said Simon. He looked at me and smiled like an evil and sinister lunatic.

"Give me the information," Justine said.

I cut my eyes at her and handed her the bogus information.

Justine smiled and said, "We'll be right back."

"How could you let him say those things to me?" I demanded.

"Girl, he was just playing around with you. Stop being so sensitive," she said as she grabbed her large red pocketbook off the table. "Now we'll be back in a little while."

"Are you sure you're coming back?" I asked thinking that Justine was about to pull a move and leave me stuck with my baby stepbrother. It wouldn't have been the first time that she'd disappeared on me.

"Don't worry. I am coming back, Keysha. Simon and I have to make a quick run, that's all. Watch Flip for me, okay?"

"So, what now, I'm your built-in babysistter? I don't want to watch him," I snapped at her. I was enraged by her choosing Simon over me.

"Keysha, I promise we will not be long. We'll be back in less than an hour," she said but I didn't believe a single word passing through her lying lips.

"Where are you going?" I asked.

"To handle some business real quick. Just do what I said and everything will be fine. I'm tired of you always questioning me! If you keep on prying into my business I'm going to pop you on the mouth!" Justine viciously yelled at me and then gave me an evil look just before she rushed out the door.

"She's driving me crazy!" I growled out. I went over and sat down on the sofa and placed my face in my hands. "This is so stupid. Everything about this jacked-up situation is stupid." I pulled out my cell phone and gave Wesley a call.

"Hey, Wesley," I said when answered the phone.

"Hey, Keysha."

Wesley didn't sound like himself. I could tell that something was wrong. "Are you okay? You don't sound too good," I said.

"Keysha, some stuff has happened," Wesley said.

"Stuff? What stuff? What are you talking about? What's all of that noise in the background? It sounds like police sirens," I said.

"Keysha, I've got to go. I'll call you back. I've got to go handle something," he said.

"Handle something. What are you talking about? Are you in trouble, Wesley? Hello—Hello? I can't believe he hung up on me," I said aloud as I tried to call him right back but I didn't get an answer. "What the hell!" I said as I tried to dial him once again. I still got no answer. I paced the floor and tried to call Wesley back for at least thirty minutes but he wouldn't answer his phone.

"What is going on? Has the world and everyone in it suddenly gone crazy?" I wondered.

Just as I was about to call Wesley yet again, Justine burst into the apartment with a crazed look in her eyes.

"Come on, Keysha, let's go," she said as she rushed over to Flip and quickly scooped him up. Just as she leaned forward the large purse she was carrying opened up and I noticed that there were bundles of paper wrapped money in it. While Justine wrestled with Flip some of the stacks spilled and fell to the floor. "Come on, girl, and get the molasses out of your ass. Pick up that money and let's go! Simon is outside waiting in a car!"

"What's going on?" I was confused and almost in hysterics.

"What does it look like, girl? We're getting the hell out of Dodge!" she said.

"I'm not going anywhere with you and that pervert!" I screamed at her.

"Keysha, I don't have time for this. Now we're going to take this money and that account information and get the hell out of town so that we can start over. Come on now. I told you there was a big payday in all of this for you. Here's your chance to score big."

"What did you do? Rob a bank?" I asked, fearful of the answer I'd get. Justine picked up the stacks of money and headed toward the door but I quickly beat her to the door and stood in her path.

"Move, Keysha!" she barked at me.

"No. Now answer me. Did you rob a bank?" I asked more forcefully.

"No. The Currency Exchange is a few blocks over. It's the one next to the liquor store and the First Baptist Church," she said and walked around me and out into the hallway.

"Mom. Stop! Think about what you're doing. You don't have to do this. You have a choice. Take the money back. Simon is no good for you and you know this. Once your money runs out, he's going to put you on a street corner and you know it!" Justine paused in thought for a moment and I tried to grab her pocketbook but she wrestled it away from me.

"This is my half of the money and I'm not going to let you or anyone else take it," she yelled at me and started speed walking down the hall toward the exit.

I followed her, pleading. "Please. Mom, don't do this."

I was hoping to talk some sense into her. The moment we stepped outside of the building, we paused momentarily and listened to the wail of police sirens drawing near.

"Come on! We've got to go. The police are coming!" Simon yelled out the car window. "Why are you two playing around? If you don't get in this car I'm pulling the hell off. I'm not going back to jail!"

"She's not going with you, Simon!" I shouted at him like a deranged woman who'd lost her mind.

"Yes, I am," Justine walked down the steps with the baby in one arm and the oversize bag lodged between her arm and torso. I tried to snatch the bag from her again but couldn't get it.

"Justine, stop. I'm trying to save you from yourself!" I tried talking a little more calmly hoping she would reconsider what she was doing.

"Keysha, look, it's not going to matter when we steal Jordan and Barbara's identity and drain their bank accounts. Their money is insured by the bank. They'll get it back. Why are you being so hardheaded about this?"

I glared at my mother for a long moment. My hate and contempt for her had surfaced and I no longer wanted to save her as much as I wanted to save Jordan and Barbara from her and Simon's treachery. "The account information is bogus, Mom. I made up the information. I was hoping to talk you out of doing this."

"What? You lied to me? You didn't get it? How could you do this to me? Do you know what I went through to get this money? This money and that account information were going to be used to help us start over, Keysha! How could you betray me like this? You're supposed be on my side!"

Simon began horn honking again. "I'm not about to listen to you two fight about this. I'm pulling off!" Simon said as he jerked the car into gear. When Justine ducked inside of the car I lunged for her purse and tried once again to wrestle it from her. During our struggle several stacks of the paper-wrapped money fell to the ground. After Justine took a swing at me she secured her purse and told Simon, "Let's get the hell out of here!" Simon pressed the gas pedal so hard that the tires squealed as the car pulled off. I picked up the stacks of money and rushed back inside the building trying to figure out what to do next. A few moments later a parade of squad cars zoomed down the block at a high rate of speed. I knew that it wouldn't be long before Justine and Simon were caught.

I rushed back inside the apartment, dropped the bundles of money on the floor and sat on the sofa. I wanted to cry but I was too angry to shed any tears.

"Why did you try to grab the bag, Keysha?" I asked myself over and over again. At that moment I decided to call Jordan but I couldn't get through to him. His phone went directly to voice mail. I then decided that the best thing to do was to walk up to the Currency Exchange and return the money. My biggest desire was to remain with Jordan, Barbara and Mike. The last thing I wanted was to jeopardize my ability to remain in the house with them by being accused of helping Justine and Simon pull off a robbery. I prayed that the police would believe my story. I picked up the money and placed it all inside of my bag which was just big enough to hold it all. I figured that by the time I walked up there, the police would have cornered and arrested both Justine and Simon for their crime. As I prepared to leave. I pressed the Redial button and tried to reach Jordan again.

sixteen

MIKE
Saturday, March 1st

I was hoping that the urge to go to the bathroom would go away because I wanted to sleep a little longer. I ignored the need to go for as long as I could and then finally had to get up and answer nature's call. Once I was done in the bathroom, I walked down to Keysha's room to see if she was in there. I wanted to tell her about the wild time I'd had the night before. I pushed open her door, took one look at her orderly room and knew that she wasn't in there. I don't know how she manages to keep her room as clean as she does but she certainly does a better job of it than I do. I need to get with her program so that my mom doesn't have to come in to clean my room and run across my stash of condoms. I went back into my room and sat at my messy desk, which was filled with magazines and assignments from school. I booted up my computer. As I waited, I began to think about the party I'd gone to last night. I told my parents that I was going to Marlon's birthday party but I actually went to a juke jam at a place called 5th City in Chicago. I knew that my parents would never let me go to a place like that filled with unsupervised teenagers from all over the city. Oh, no, that just would not have happened if I'd told them where I was really going.

While I was there, I hooked up with Sabrina who'd also told a lie to her parents in order to go. She'd once again hooked up with Katina and had Katina's older sister drive her over and drop her off. I'd decided to let Sabrina off the hook a little to see if she'd learned her lesson which was that she shouldn't get me all worked up and then fake me out. Besides, I changed my thinking a little bit. I figured that having two girls is better than just having one. I could have a girl in the suburbs and a girl in the city. I knew the likelihood of Toya and Sabrina ever meeting each other was slim to none.

My computer finally came up so I typed in my password. I then stretched my arms up high above my head, yawned and folded my arms across my chest. Last night, I had to admit, was one of the wildest times I'd ever had. Once I was out of the house, I'd hooked up with Marlon and Romeo who were both eagerly anticipating a great night of dancing and meeting girls. Although both Marlon and Romeo had girlfriends, their ladies wouldn't be with us tonight.

"I can't believe you told Sabrina about this party,"

Romeo said who was sitting in the back seat of Marlon's Navigator. "Dude, you're bringing sand to the beach." Both Romeo and Marlon laughed.

"Hey, she might not even show up. She has to jump through a lot of hoops just to get out of the house," I said.

"Whatever, man. That girl is going to show up," Marlon said as he got onto the entrance ramp for the highway. "You need to get a better understanding with her so that she doesn't begin to think that every time you go somewhere she is supposed to come with you."

"It's not even like that. This will be the first time that Sabrina and I have hooked up in weeks." I'd gotten a little defensive.

"Dude, she's a manager for the track team just so that she can watch you run. Admit it. She's a fatal attraction," said Marlon.

"Maybe she is and maybe she isn't. I don't know," I said.

"Why do you want to hook up with her at a party like this where there's going to be honeys all over the place shaking their behinds and doing all kinds of freaky stuff on the dance floor? You'll probably get at least fifteen to twenty phone numbers tonight."

"What? You guys think Sabrina is the only girl I've got in the stable?" I asked.

"Yeah," they both said at the same time and then laughed.

"Well, that's where you guys are wrong! Just dead wrong."

"Well, do tell, because inquiring minds want to know," said Marlon pressing the accelerator and causing the big Navigator to zoom down the highway at a faster pace.

"I've got a girl on the south side of the city. Her name is Toya," I said.

"Mike, quit lying," said Romeo.

"Dude, I'm telling you the truth," I said.

"How old is she?" asked Marlon.

"Seventeen," I said.

"Boy, please. You cannot pull a seventeen-year-old girl!" said Marlon.

"Well, I'm telling you differently. Last time I saw her was about two weeks ago," I said.

"What street does she live on?" asked Romeo.

"Right off of King Drive," I said.

"How did you get way down there from the suburbs?" Marlon asked.

"Public transportation," I said.

"Oh, no. Old girl isn't going to be kicking with you for too long. She's just playing with you right now until some dude with a ride comes along."

"No, she isn't, man. I'm telling you. She doesn't mind catching the bus, plus she's setting it out," I bragged.

"What?" Romeo perked up. "How far have you gotten with her?" he asked.

"I almost hit a homerun but her grandmother came home."

"Yeah, right," Marlon said as he chuckled.

"I'm serious, man. I've never kissed lips as soft as hers

or felt a behind as soft as hers. I'm telling you guys. It was like touching floating clouds."

"What does she look like?" asked Romeo.

"She's nice-looking. She's light-skinned, with long black hair. Nice breasts and a juicy booty."

"Okay, so what's the catch?" asked Marlon. "There has to be something up with this girl. Is she slow or something?"

"No, she's not slow," I said.

"Then how did you meet her?" asked Marlon

"She's a friend of Keysha's. I met her when we had to drop Keysha off to visit with her mom. Shorty saw me standing in the hallway and just walked all up on me talking noise."

"She must have a baby," Marlon said.

"Yeah. How did you know that?" I asked.

"Okay, that explains it. Shorty is going to try and open up your nose real quick. You be careful with Toya," Marlon said. "I'm serious. When you get down with her make sure you're protected. I don't want to hear any excuses about her being pregnant with your baby."

"Man, I'm not even going out like that. I keep a raincoat with me," I boasted.

"Yo, turn that song up," Romeo said to Marlon. Marlon turned up the song and we cruised down the highway listing to the song "Lollipop" by Lil' Wayne.

When we arrived at 5th City, we drove past the building and saw a massive crowd of people standing outside waiting to get in.

"Oh, man. Look at that line!" said Romeo. "We're not going to get in," he complained.

"We're going to get in. My cousin is the bouncer," said Marlon who'd pulled out his cell phone and made a call. "Yo, Pee Wee," Marlon greeted his cousin on the phone. "It's Marlon. We just got here. I'm about to park. Okay. Come to the front door and you'll walk us in? Cool," Marlon said and then hung up the phone. "No problem, guys. We're in."

Once we parked the car, we walked back toward the building with a crowd of other partygoers. The line literally snaked around the building. People were standing outside in their coats bundled up trying to stay warm while they waited. Marlon, Romeo and I walked past the crowds and right up to the door where Pee Wee was standing.

"That's Pee Wee?" I asked. Marlon's cousin was a goliath of a man. He was massive. He stood about six-foot-eight, weighed at least three hundred pounds and looked meaner than the devil himself.

"What's up, boy?" Pee Wee greeted Marlon.

"Nothing, man. Just hoping to get a little lucky tonight," Marlon answered.

"Did you park your daddy's Navigator in the parking lot around back like I told you to?" asked Pee Wee.

"Yeah, I did," answered Marlon.

"Cool. Come on. I'll walk ya'll in." Pee Wee turned around and led us through the massive crowds of people. As soon as we stepped inside, we walked forward and up a few stairs. There was even a line of people on the inside waiting to pay the entrance fee.

"Look at all of the honeys in here tonight." Romeo checked all of the ladies who were waiting in line. "Woo, it's going to be a good night," he said as he clapped his hands together.

"Yeah, there are some hot-looking girls in here," I agreed with Romeo.

"I seriously hope that you learn a little lesson from this. Don't ever, ever, ever bring sand to the beach," Romeo said as he began laughing.

"Forget you, man. Your luck may not be so good tonight," I said.

"Dude, you'd have to be a complete idiot if you came in here tonight and didn't get lucky," said Romeo.

We walked through a set of brown doors and past several girls who were standing around talking on their cell phones. We walked through another set of doors that had a No Smoking sign posted above it and into a very large dance hall. The place was jam-packed. The music was loud and all I could see was a sea of people gyrating with wild abandon to the music of Missy Elliott. I couldn't help but get caught up in the rhythm of the music.

"This is what I'm talking about!" Marlon yelled out over the loud noise of the music and the choirs of voices shouting and singing along. A moment later, I felt a tap on my shoulder. I turned around and saw Sabrina and Katina.

"Hey, baby!" Sabrina wasted no time wrapping her arms around me and planting a kiss on me. I took her into my embrace and enjoyed our moment together.

"I've been waiting on you," she said as she took my hand and led me out to the crowded dance floor.

"Yo, I'll catch up with y'all later," I said to Marlon and Romeo who were standing around admiring all the girls who were working their behinds. I thought that Sabrina was the only girl with me but once I started dancing I realized that Katina had also joined us. We danced and sweated until our backs and knees ached. We jumped around, bounced around and tossed our hands in the air as the chorus of voices sang along with the music. At one point, Sabrina once again shook her behind like a pair of pom-poms and got me worked up. But this time I didn't have any expectations so I was cool with it, especially since there were other girls standing next to us shaking their behinds just as hard. It wasn't long before the girls had sweated out every curl on their head. Sabrina, Katina and I danced and jumped around for about an hour without taking a break. Then, just as the party was kicking into high gear, the DJ made an announcement.

"The Chicago Police are here and they're shutting us down, y'all."

Everyone in the place started booing.

"I know. I know," said the DJ. "They say we have too many people in here and it's a fire-code violation. On top of that, there are even more people outside waiting to get in. So, that's just the way it goes, y'all. We've been told to shut the music off and send everyone home."

At that moment everyone started yelling out. "We're not leaving! We're not leaving!" It was a coordinated act of pure defiance.

"We'd better get out of here," I said. "This is going to turn ugly." Sabrina, Katina and I made our way to the front door and outside. Once outside, we saw police there with squad-car lights flashing everywhere. They'd blocked off the street and had paddy wagons lined up to arrest anyone who got out of hand.

"Come on, let's get out of here," said Marlon, who'd just exited the club with Romeo.

"Wait a minute. Do you guys need a ride back?" I asked Sabrina.

"Katina is on the phone with her sister now," she said. We waited for a moment for Katina to finish her call.

"Can you give us a ride back?" asked Katina. "My sister is on the other side of town and won't be back this way for at least an hour." All of a sudden out of nowhere people started yelling about a fight inside the dance hall.

"Come on, it's time to go," said Marlon.

We all rushed around the building toward the parking lot but were stopped cold in our tracks when a massive wave of people came running toward us crying out, "They've pulled out the police dogs! The police dogs are out!" My natural instinct told me to turn around and run with the crowd but Marlon said, "Come on. Let's get to the car!" We all rushed against the crowd toward the parking lot. There were so many people running toward us that I got separated from Marlon, Sabrina, Katina and Romeo. As I struggled against a mob of people, I came face to face with an officer and a barking police dog.

"Ah!" I yelled out as the dog lunged for my manhood and attempted to bite it off. The police held the dog back but the large German shepherd kept lunging for me.

"Get that dog, man!" I yelled at the officer.

"Go home!" the officer ordered.

"I'm trying to, man! Call that dog off!" I pleaded with him. The officer calmed the dog down and I continued on my way trying to maneuver through the crowd. I caught up with the group and got into the car.

"Where did you go?" asked Sabrina.

"A complaint should be filed against the police department for turning those dogs lose on people," I said with an angry voice.

"Baby, what happened?" Sabrina began rubbing my back in an effort to calm me down.

"Nothing," I said. "I just hate the police. I never want to get in trouble with the police." Not long after that, all kinds of mayhem between the police and the crowd broke lose. The police shot tear gas into the mob to help disperse them. At that point, Marlon cranked up the car and drove through an exit at the rear of the parking.

The sound of my cell phone ringing startled me. I quickly searched through my bed sheets to see who was calling me so early in the morning. Once I found my phone I saw that Toya was trying to reach me.

"Hello," I said.

"Hey, baby. I haven't seen you in a while and I wanted to know if you'd come see me today," Toya said seductively. I smiled as I lay down on my bed and rubbed on my stomach.

"You want me to roll through today?" I asked, knowing full well that she'd said that.

"I've been thinking about you every day, Mike. I can't wait anymore."

"I don't know if I can make it down there today. I didn't plan on it."

"Mike, I'm wearing the purple panties that you brought for me right now. Just come on down real quick. Please."

"Dang, girl, you sound like you're on fire," I said, liking the idea that she was begging me to come see her.

"What if I am?"

"Are you?" I asked.

"Come on down and I'll show you," she said.

"It's going to take me at least two hours to get down there, Toya." I said as I walked over to my computer and began looking up the train schedule.

"Can't you just drive the Trans Am down? You'll get here much quicker. My grandmother has already left with my son and she'll be gone for at least five hours. And I know your parents are gone because I saw them drop Keysha off and overheard them talking about going to the auto show all day. So Mike. Are you going to come see me so that I can give you my sweet love? Or are you going to chicken out?" Toya asked.

Something came over me when she said that. Something inside told me that sometimes you just got to do what you've to do and deal with the consequences later. Then I thought, I'd already driven the Trans Am once and got away with it. Jordan didn't even notice. Then I thought. If I pulled it off once, I could most certainly pull it off twice.

"No." I said. "I'm not going to chicken out on you. I'll be there in about thirty minutes," I said.

"Good. I'll be in my bed waiting on you," she said and then hung up the phone. I quickly sprung into action. I called my parents to confirm that they were going to be at the auto show all day. Once that was confirmed I took a shower, put on some clothes and grabbed seventy-five dollars from my stash of cash. I grabbed four condoms, I didn't know how many opportunities I'd get, and rushed downstairs. I grabbed the keys for the Trans Am, went out to the garage, fired it up and pulled off. I made sure that I obeyed every rule of the road because the last thing I wanted or needed was to be pulled over by the police who would love nothing more than to beat my black behind for driving without a driver's license or permit.

When I arrived at Toya's apartment building, I parked the car in the vacant lot on the side of the building so that Jordan wouldn't see it in case he returned early or something to pick up Keysha. I walked inside the building with another tenant and rushed down the hallway to Toya's door. I drummed against the door with my knuckles. True to her word, when Toya opened the door, she was wearing nothing but a robe and the purple panty-and-bra set which I'd purchased for her. I stood with my mouth open for a moment because it marked the very first time I'd ever seen a girl that naked outside of a video clip on YouTube.

"Do you like it?" Toya asked.

"Oh yeah," I said as I stepped inside the apartment. I was about to take off my coat and get right down to business but Toya stopped me.

"Where's the car?" she asked innocently.

"Out back," I said.

"Well, can I see it?" she asked.

"There's nothing to see. It's just a car. You can see it later after we—"

"Come on. Just let me see it, baby. It will only take five minutes. What's five minutes when we have five hours? Don't worry. You're going to get everything you've got coming to you," she said. "See?" Toya removed her robe and turned around so that I could get a better look. "Touch my body," she said. I placed my hand on her voluptuous behind, closed my eyes and exhaled loudly.

"See. It's not going anywhere and you're going to have it all to yourself in a minute. Now, just wait here while I put on some jeans and a top real quick."

"Okay," I said. Toya returned a few moments later

fully dressed. When we stepped into the hallway, I heard Keysha yelling and shouting at her mother.

"Come on. We'll go out the back way," Toya said. We walked out of the rear exit that let out at an alley. We walked around to the vacant lot where the car was parked.

"Oh, my god. It's a beautiful car!" Toya said aloud as we approached. I opened up the door so that she could see the inside of it.

"Oh, this is so nice, Mike." She seemed more excited about the car than she did about seeing me. "Promise you'll take me for a spin in it before you leave?"

"Yeah. I promise," I said smiling at Toya.

"Good. You can drive me past my girlfriend's house. I'm going to call her real quick to let her know that I'll be dropping by later." Toya pulled out her cell phone and made a quick call.

"Yeah, he has the classic Trans Am. I'm going to roll by in it later," I heard her say before she hung up the phone.

"Okay, Mike. Let's go back inside and do this," said Toya. I locked the car back up and walked back inside with Toya. Once we were inside her apartment again, we walked back to her bedroom.

"Get completely undressed," she said as she turned on a small radio situated next to her bed. She turned the music up kind of loud.

"We don't want the neighbors to hear us. These walls are very thin," she said.

I didn't waste any time stripping down to my underwear or leaping into her bed. Toya picked up my clothes off the floor.

"I'm going to set your clothes up front on the sofa and then I'll be right in," she said.

"I have some condoms in my front pants pocket. Bring them with you when you come back," I said.

"I found the car keys," she said.

"Look in the other pocket for the condoms," I yelled out.

"Okay," she answered back.

I laid on the bed with my eyes closed. Excited to be there and filled with wild anticipation. I threaded my fingers behind my head and smiled at the thought of losing my virginity today.

"Toya, where you at, girl? What's taking so long?" I called out but didn't get a response.

"Toya?" I called out her name again but still got no response. Something didn't feel right, so I got out of the bed and walked back to the front of the apartment.

"Toya?" I called out again. I thought she might have stepped out into the hallway so I opened the door. I could still hear Keysha down the hall yelling and shouting. I looked in the direction of her mother's apartment and saw the door opening.

"She's right these walls are thin," I whispered as I ducked back inside the apartment and shut the door.

"Toya?" I called her again thinking that she was perhaps in the bathroom. As I stood there looking at my clothes on the sofa, I was perplexed until I heard the motor of the Trans Am being fired up.

"No!" I shouted out as I rushed over to the sofa to put my pants on

"No! Toya!" I screamed out as I stuffed my feet into my shoes, put on my shirt, grabbed my coat and rushed out of the building.

"Toya, no!" I ran down the back stairs and out of the rear exit. I rushed around to the side of the building and I yelled out "Come back!" as Toya and some man sped away in Jordan's car. I ran after them but it was too late. They were gone.

seventeen

KEYSHA
Saturday, March 1st

I was a nervous wreck after Justine flipped on me. I couldn't believe she'd set me up like this. I called Jordan but the phone went directly to voice mail again. I figured that he probably couldn't get a signal inside the massive convention center. I paced the floor of the apartment for a minute and then finally mustered up enough courage to go with my original plan and take the money back to the Currency Exchange and explain my story. I'd explain how my mother had just robbed them and how I stopped her from getting away with their money. It was the best plan that I could think of in my frazzled state of mind. I found a black trash bag nestled between the refrigerator and the countertop. I opened up the trash bag and placed the bank pouch inside. I tied a knot in the bag then rushed out of the apartment building. As I was coming out of the building, I saw Mike sprinting out from the vacant lot of land next to the building. He looked completely disoriented.

"Mike?" I called out his name. He glanced in the direction of my voice. There was a wild look in his eyes that I'd never seen before.

"Keysha!" He called out to me as if he'd just been shot or something. The terror in his voice shook my soul. Mike ran over to me, out of breath, confused, bewildered and unsettled.

"Something horrible has happened," he said as he crumbled to his knees.

"Mike, what's wrong, are you hurt?" I asked as I quickly checked him for any sign of trauma. Mike started tearing up.

"She stole it from me, Keysha," he cried out in emotional pain.

"Stole what? What are doing down here, Mike?" I fired off a series of questions at him once I realized he wasn't bleeding to death.

"Oh, God, I've messed up. I've messed up big time. Jordan and Barbara are going to kill me." Mike just burst into tears.

"Mike! Pull yourself together, boy, and tell me what happened."

Mike smeared away the tears from his face and sucked down his pain. "That bitch Toya stole Jordan's car! She took the Trans Am," Mike said.

"Wait a minute. Let me get this straight. Have you been secretly doing Toya?" I asked.

"Yeah, Keysha. That's why I'm down here," he admitted.

"Oh, I don't believe this." I said as I sat down on a step. I sat the plastic bag of money down by my side and placed my face in my hands. "You drove Jordan's Trans Am all the way down here to impress her!"

"It's a little more complicated than that, Keysha." Mike explained. "She promised to take my—to take my virginity away if I drove the car down here to see her."

"You did all of this over her stanky booty?" I couldn't believe that Mike was so blinded. "Mike, I told you that Toya was a snake! I told you that her boyfriend was into stealing cars!"

"I don't remember you saying that," Mike said.

"The first day you met her I said that. But you were too busy gawking at her jiggling booty and jiggling breasts."

"Do you think they'll bring the car back?" he asked.

"Boy. That car and Toya are gone. She's not coming back anytime soon. Once they sell that car, they're going to get a lot of money and they're going to disappear for a little while. That's how Toya gets down," I said.

"What about her baby? And school? And her grandmother?" Mike asked.

"Ooh, boy, you don't have a single clue at all! Toya doesn't give two cents about her baby. Her blind grandmother has been taking care of her baby because Toya is crazy. Second, Toya is a high-school dropout!"

"I didn't know," Mike said.

"Of course you didn't. You're so full of sperm that you didn't even think to check out what she was really about. All you wanted to do was get your jollies," I scolded him.

"What am I going to do, Keysha? When Jordan finds out he's going to snap me in half! I might as well pack my bags and run away now."

"You know, you've got to deal with it. I've got my own drama to deal with right now. I've got to take this money back," I said and stood up.

"Money? What money? What are you talking about?" he asked.

"My mother and that dumb ass Simon have robbed the damn Currency Exchange a few blocks over. Right now they're out somewhere being chased by the police. I'm going to go take this money back," I said as I started to leave.

"Keysha, please wait. Help me. What am I supposed to do?" Mike looked incredibly pitiful. "Should I just kill myself now?" Mike began hyperventilating.

"I don't know. I don't have any answers to your problem," I said.

"Maybe I can go steal the car back. Do you have any idea where they might have taken the car?" Mike asked. I stopped and paused for a minute. I searched my memory to see if I could remember anything I may have overheard at some point.

"They're probably anticipating you calling the police so they can't drive too far in that car. I have heard that car thieves have a special hideaway over on 51st Street near the old stockyards, but that was a while ago."

"Come go with me, Keysha." Mike pleaded. "I don't know where that is."

"Mike, I have to take this money back," I said.

"Keysha, please, this is life or death. If the car is there, we'll get it back, then we'll bring the money back and go home."

"And how am I supposed to explain how I got home?" I asked him.

"Tell them that Justine freaked out and you caught Metra train back home. By the time we get home, you can call them so that they don't make an extra trip back here. Please, Keysha. I'm begging you. I was there for you when all of that mess with Liz went down. You owe me. Please help me fix this."

How could I not help him after he'd brought up Liz Lloyd? I felt as if I was being pulled in several directions at once.

"Please, Keysha." Mike begged me again.

"Okay," I exhaled. "But how are we going to get the car back if it's there?" I asked.

"I'll figure it out when I get there," Mike said.

"Come on," I said. "We can catch a cab over to the place I'm talking about."

I had the cab driver drop us off two blocks away from the old stockyards so that we wouldn't alarm anyone. Mike and I wandered cautiously around, peeping inside the windows of old abandoned structures where livestock were once slaughtered and then shipped off the supermarkets. The stockyards had been closed for years but the old structures were never demolished. The area was a haven for back-alley deals, payoffs to dirty cops and other illegal activities.

"I don't know, Mike. It doesn't look like they're here and this place is creeping me out," I said.

"Let's just check the last building ahead of us." The last structure was about one hundred yards in front of us. There were no other buildings around so anyone who looked out a window would see us coming.

"I've got a bad feeling about this, Mike," I said.

"Come on, Keysha. Please," Mike said. "On the count of three, we're going to run over there. Okay?" Mike wanted me to confirm that I'd run with him across the open lot that was littered with old railroad tracks, old train cars, broken chunks of concrete and other abandoned wreckage.

"Okay," I said.

"One, two, three, go!" Mike counted down and we ran as fast as we could to the last structure. When we got there, we rested our backs against the old dilapidated building. There was an open window above our heads so Mike stood up and peeked inside.

"It's here," Mike whispered loudly. He was clearly excited about finding the car.

"For real?" I asked.

"Yes," Mike said peeping back inside. "There are several cars in there. Jordan's car is just on the other side of this wall," Mike whispered. "And the keys are still in the ignition. There are several dudes at the other end of the building talking. I see Toya's stanky butt as well," Mike said as he ducked back down.

"Okay. I've had enough of this *Harriet the Spy* and *Scooby Doo* crap. I'm calling the police," I said and reached for my cell phone.

"No!" Mike stopped me.

"What do you mean, no?" I said. "We've found the car, Mike. Let's call the police and get this over with."

"Call the police after we get Jordan's car back," Mike said.

"Mike, how are you going to get in there? Those guys probably have guns and you can't stop a bullet. You're not bulletproof."

"I've got to try, Keysha. I've got to fix this. Once I get the car back, believe me, I am going to straight chill out. I'm just going to focus on school and focus on being a good son. I've never been in this type of trouble with my parents, Keysha. All of the deception I've been pulling lately is not going to go over well with them."

"Oh, God. What have you gotten me into, Mike?" I asked as I weighed our options and considered his plan. Mike looked around for an entrance.

"Look, over there. There is a door that's cracked open. Come on." Mike said and moved toward the door before I could stop him. He gently pulled open the old, rusty and squeaky metal door. He opened it up just enough for both of us to squeeze through it. We crouched down as low as we could and raced over to Jordan's Trans Am.

Mike opened the door on the driver's side very quietly and very slowly. Once it was open enough, he turned to me and whispered.

"Crawl in!" I did what he asked and made my way to the passenger seat. Once I was inside, I fastened my seat belt. Mike got in and gently pulled the door shut.

"I sure hope you know how to drive this car good," I whispered. Mike looked out the window past me at Toya who saw that we were in the car. Mike gave her and the men the middle finger and started up the motor. He put the car in Drive and slammed down on the accelerator. The tires of the powerful muscle car squealed as the car moved forward and fishtailed. Mike quickly gained control over the car and rushed toward the exit where Toya, Junior's father and a few other men were standing. Everyone leaped out of the way as Mike bolted through the exit and made a hard left. The car did a power slide sending all kinds of lose rocks, dust and other debris flying into the air.

"Go!" I shouted at him as I looked out the back window to see if the bad guys had guns. Mike didn't continue driving and I wondered why. When I turned back and saw what he saw, my heart stopped.

"Oh, no. This can't be happening!" Mike screamed out. Squad cars from the Chicago Police Department where rushing toward us with their lights flashing and sirens wailing.

"I hate the police!" Mike said and slammed down on the accelerator. The Trans Am responded immediately.

The motor howled, the tires screamed and the car began moving out.

"Mike! What are you doing?" I screamed at him.

"We're going home, Keysha! I'm not going to get into trouble for this!" he said as he swerved to avoid hitting a squad car. Mike lost control of the powerful muscle car which spun around and finally stopped when the rear quarter panel crashed into a wooden utility pole.

"Damn it!" Mike tried to start the car but it wouldn't turn over. He looked at me and said "Come on. Let's run!" Mike opened up his car door.

"Mike, stop," I said as I rubbed the side of my head which had slammed against the passenger door window.

"Come on, Keysha, we can run away from this! We'll just tell a lie to Jordan that the car was stolen from the garage. I don't want to tell my Dad that I wrecked his car! He loves this car. He probably loves this car more than he loves me. He's going to kill me, Keysha. I'd rather the police shoot me dead now instead of facing Jordan and the consequences." Mike rambled not wanting to concede to the fact that we were both in some major trouble.

"Mike," I said as I touched his shoulder. "We're already in way over our heads. Your running away is only going to make it worse than what it is. Especially if you panic now." At that moment the police surrounded the car and barricaded us in. They drew their weapons on us and told us to get out of the car slowly. Mike got out of the car first with hands above his head. The police instructed him to lie facedown on the ground. Once they had Mike in handcuffs, they instructed me to get out of the car and do the same. Once I was down on the cold ground, an officer placed my wrists in handcuffs. Mike and I were pulled to our feet then other officers began searching the car. I noticed that other officers were also in the process of arresting Toya and everyone else she was associated with. The entire moment felt like a scene from a Hollywood movie but it wasn't fiction, it was real and it didn't make me feel good at all.

"Looks like we've found some of the money that was stolen from the Currency Exchange earlier today," said the officer, who'd just found my purse and opened it up.

"Wait. I can explain that," I said hastily.

"Well, before you do, let me read you your Miranda Rights," said the officer who'd just finished searching my purse. "You have the right to remain silent and refuse to answer questions. Anything you do or say may be used against you in a court of law. You have the right to consult an attorney before speaking to the police and to have an attorney present during the questioning if you wish. If you decide to answer questions now without an attorney present you will still have the right to stop answering questions at any time until you talk to an attorney. Knowing and understanding your rights as I have explained them to you, are you willing to answer my questions without an attorney present?"

"Can I ask you a question?" I asked the officer as I

glanced over at Mike, who had his head slumped down between his shoulders. He looked so defeated and worn out.

"What's your question?" the officer asked.

"Can I call my Dad?" I asked as tears began streaming down my cheeks.

eighteen

MIKE
Saturday, March 1st

I sat handcuffed in the back of the police squad car, looking out the window at Toya, who was also being arrested. Once officers placed her inside the police car she was quickly driven away. I thought that she'd attempt to catch a glimpse of me as she was passing by, but Toya didn't so much as glance in my direction.

"Why, you cheap tramp? Why did you do this to me?" I yelled out as the car continued on its way. I tried to hold my tears back but I couldn't. I cried so hard that my chest began hurting. I was a total mess in desperate need of some tissue so that I could blow my nose. The officers on the scene didn't seem to care about my misery or my dilemma. They were too busy making sure they'd rounded up everyone. It wasn't long before an army of trucks showed up and began the process of towing away all the cars. I watched as Jordan's Trans Am was dragged into position so that it could be mounted to a tow truck. Once it was angled properly, the tow-truck driver, who was an overweight man wearing a mechanic's uniform covered with oil stains, placed tow hooks beneath the rear of the tow truck and flipped a lever. I watched in horror as the Trans Am was hoisted high in the air.

"Be careful!" I cried, but no one could hear me.

The tow-truck driver then got in the cab and took off at a high speed, causing the nose of the Trans Am to bounce violently against the concrete.

I placed my head against the window of the squad car and continued to cry. Over the past few weeks, I'd prided myself on being both physically and emotionally strong, but at this moment my crumbling emotions were winning the fight over my self-control. At that moment I prayed for God to end my life so that my suffering would end. I wanted to die so that I wouldn't have to face the consequences of the mess I'd got myself into.

A fair amount of time passed before an officer got in the squad car and told me that he was taking me to the police station, where I'd be processed and detained. By that point I didn't care much about anything that happened to me. The world around me seemed to be moving in slow motion. My state of mind was confused and incoherent. It was as if a megaton bomb went off in my heart and the aftermath of the explosion left an eerie stillness and silence.

We arrived at the police station about thirty minutes

later and I was brought in through an entrance at the rear of the building. I was escorted through a series of giant and impenetrable doors and was finally asked to stop in front of a long countertop where several officers were working.

"Hey, Monique. Can I get some paperwork so that I can process this guy?" said the officer who'd brought me in to the female officer behind the counter. Once Monique gave him what he'd asked for, he walked me over to a desk and sat me down.

"Sir," I spoke directly to the officer.

"Hmm?" he asked as he began filling out a form that was attached to a clipboard.

"My name is Mike Kendall. I know I'm in trouble and will not be leaving anytime soon. But I was just wondering if you could walk me to the bathroom so that I can clean up my face." The officer stopped writing the glanced at me for a moment. I could tell that he was trying to determine if I was worth the effort of going out of his way to be nice. "I'm not going to run or anything. I just want to get cleaned up." I assured him.

"My name is Detective O'Malley," he said and then set the clipboard on the desk. "Stand up and follow me," he said and then escorted me to the bathroom.

"Okay. Go on in and make it quick," he instructed me.

It felt good to splash cold water on my face and erase the tears and dirt. "Thanks," I said, once I was back in the hallway.

"Mike, I'm going to place you in a holding cell while

I run a background check on you," said Detective O'Malley as he looked at my State Identification Card, which he had pulled from my wallet.

"Okay. I understand," I said and followed him into a small concrete room with no windows and a solid door.

"Have a seat. I'll be back," he said and then locked me inside. I sat down, placed my face in my hands and tried to reassure myself that everything was going to be okay. A long time passed before Detective O'Malley returned.

"Come on. I'm going to allow you to make a phone call," he said.

"Thank you," I said and followed him over to an empty desk where there was a black telephone. I swallowed hard before I picked it up and dialed.

"Hello," I heard Grandmother Katie's soothing voice. She sounded so pleasant and gentle.

"Hello," I uttered before a wave of sadness gripped me.

"Mike, is that you? What's wrong? Why are you upset?" she asked, filled with loving concern.

"I'm in trouble," I answered her. "I didn't want to call Jordan because he'd going to kill me when he finds out what has happened." I said, struggling to gain my composure.

"Mike. Your father isn't going to kill you." She tried to assure me. "Now tell me what's wrong so that we can fix things. I'm sure whatever is going on it can't be all that bad."

"I'm afraid it's really bad, Grandma," I whispered.

"What happened—did someone die?" Her voice was filled with panic.

"No, not yet," I answered her.

"Stop toying with me, Mike, and tell me what's going on," she demanded.

"I'm in jail, Grandma," I answered her.

"Mike, stop playing around and tell me the truth," she said with a slight laugh, not believing that her beloved grandson was in jail.

"That is the truth. I'm in jail and I don't want to call Jordan to tell him. He's going to be so angry with me, Grandma. I've really messed up and I don't know what to do."

"Baby, what police station are you at and why are you there?"

"It's a long story, but I need your help. Will you drive up here and save me from Jordan? I want to come live you for a while."

"Mike, Jordan is not going to kill you so just calm down. Get that thought out of your head," she insisted.

"I've wrecked the Trans Am, Grandma. I smashed it up pretty badly," I said.

"Oh, boy." she sighed loudly. "Let's take this one step at a time. Does Barbara know where you are?" she asked.

"No," I answered.

"Okay. Give me that information so that I can write it down," she said. I looked over at Detective O'Malley and asked him for the address of the station. Once he gave me the information I gave it to Grandmother Katie.

"How did the car get damaged?" she asked.

"I got into an accident with it but no one was hurt," I answered her.

"Good," she said.

"Grandma, can you call Jordan and try to smooth this over with him for me? He'll listen to you." I'd just asked her for the biggest favor in my life.

"I'll see what I can do," she said. "Mike, is there someone there that I can talk to, like the arresting officer?"

"Yeah. Detective O'Malley is standing next to me," I said.

"Let me speak with him." I gave the phone to Detective O'Malley and tried to piece together the conversation he was having with Grandmother Katie but his answers were too short and direct for me to decipher anything relevant. Once he was done he said good-bye and hung up.

"Come with me," he said, and I followed him through another series of doors and into an interrogation room. Detective O'Malley told me to have a seat at the table. He then placed a folder he'd been carrying on the table and asked me if I wanted a cup of water.

"No," I said to him. Detective O'Malley sat directly across from me and opened the folder. I noticed that his hands, arms and even his cheeks had brown freckles on them. He looked about Jordan's age but had deep-set brown eyes that looked as if they'd seen a fair amount of tragedy. His eyes were stern and unyielding, and I could tell that Detective O'Malley didn't play around and wasn't the type of man who put up with foolishness. As

I took in the room I noticed the two-way mirror and wondered who was on the other side watching. I also noticed a video camera set up on a tripod in the other corner.

"Mike, you have us all puzzled here," said Detective O'Malley. "When I say all I'm also referring to my colleagues who are watching this videotaped interrogation from behind the mirror.

"We've run a background check on you and have come up with nothing. You don't have a prior record and you haven't been in trouble before. So I'm going to give you a one-time opportunity right now to come clean and explain how you ended up in the middle of a police raid." It was at that point I opened up and started talking. I laid it all out. I told Detective O'Malley about how I met Toya and the great lengths I went through to deceive my parents just so that I could get a chance to be intimate with her. I told him how my sister, Keysha, had warned me about her and insisted that I not get involved with her.

"Okay, but being stupid doesn't explain to me how you ended up over at the stockyard."

"Toya called me up and asked me to come visit her. I told her that it would take a while before I got there but she convinced me to just drive my dad's Trans Am. At the time it sounded like a great plan. I could drive down, see her and be back home before anyone noticed the car was even gone."

"So you took your father's car without his permission," asked Detective O'Malley. He glared at me and I could tell he was passing judgment on me.

"Yes," I admitted and began sobbing again.

"That's called car theft, son," he said as he scribbled down a message on a sheet of paper. He then held it up for the folks behind the mirror to see. A moment later another officer entered the room and placed a tissue box on the table before me. He then left the room.

"I know, I wasn't thinking," I said as I took a tissue and blew my nose.

"You don't even have a driver's license or permit yet," said Detective O'Malley.

"I know. I thought that since I was such a good driver, as long as I did the speed limit and obeyed the rules of the road everything would so smoothly," I explained.

"But anything could've happened. Someone could've hit you. You could've been forced to inadvertently slam into another car. You could've hurt someone. Not to mention you don't have any automobile insurance."

"I know. I didn't think about any of that when I took the car," I said.

"So, how did the car end up by the stockyard in the middle of a police raid?"

"When I got to Toya's house she wanted to see the car, so I showed it to her. Then she tricked me. She took me back inside the apartment, got me undressed and then took the car keys. When I realized that she'd set me up I ran out of the house to stop her but I was too late. She and some other guy took off in the car."

"So she turned around and stole the car that you'd stolen from your father?" Detective O'Malley was making sure that he had everything straight.

"Yes," I answered him.

"So how did you know where to find the car?" he asked.

"Keysha, my sister. Since she used to live in that neighborhood she'd heard rumors about the old stockyards being a place where thieves took cars that had been stolen." Detective O'Malley paused for a moment as he took down a few notes.

"How do you know that Keysha wasn't in on this?" he asked.

"Keysha isn't like that. She would never get involved in anything criminal." I defended my sister.

"Keysha is in another room being questioned right now. We've pulled her record and discovered that she was recently involved in a drug scandal."

"She was, but she was set up. That's all been cleared up and has nothing to do with this." I wanted to make sure Detective O'Malley understood that Keysha was innocent.

"So how did you and Keysha get over to the old stockyards?"

"We took a cab. We really didn't know what we were doing. I just wanted to see if the car was there," I said.

"And when you saw that the car was actually there, why didn't you call the police?" asked Detective O'Malley.

"Keysha wanted to call but I told her not to," I said.

"Why?" asked Detective O'Malley.

"Because. I thought I could get the car back, drive home and pretend like none of it ever happened."

"So you didn't want your parents to know what you'd been up to," said Detective O'Malley.

"That's right." I paused. "My Dad is going to kill me. I just know he is." I began tearing up once again. Detective O'Malley took a few more notes and then exited the room. I sat in there along for a very long time, trying to figure out what was going to happen to me. I thought about what my Mom and Dad would say once they were made aware of everything. The more I thought about how badly I'd messed up, the harder it became for me to contain my emotions. I crossed my arms and placed them atop of the table. I then closed my eyes and lowered my head down and rested on top of my folded arms. If I could've buried my head in the ground I would have. More time passed, and being locked up in that room was starting to drive me crazy.

"Mike, your father is here." Detective O'Malley held the door open as Jordan walked in. Jordan looked as if he couldn't believe I was actually in that room. I'd never seen an expression on his face like the one at that moment. It was filled with disappointment and grief.

"Asia, our attorney, is on her way. We're going to get this mess straightened out and then I'm going to deal with you." Jordan spoke to me in a very direct and clear tone. I knew that after this episode my life wasn't going to be the same. Jordan then walked over to me, stood behind me and rested his hands on my shoulders. I thought he was about to choke me to death but instead he massaged my shoulders, which were in knots.

"Detective O'Malley, can you tell me what the charges against my son are?" Jordan asked. Detective O'Malley asked one of his colleagues to cut off the video camera. He then entered the room and shut the door.

"Look. Mike seems like a really good kid who made a very bad judgment call and ended up at the wrong place at the wrong time. Mr. Kendall, if you don't file a police report saying that your car was stolen, we'll issue a citation for the lesser charge of joyriding. However, the car is going to remain in police custody as evidence since it was subsequently stolen from your son." Jordan inhaled deeply and then exhaled slowly. Detective O'Malley continued, "I know you want your car back, but it's going to be a while before we can turn it back over to you."

"Will this incident go on his record?" Jordan asked.

"You can speak to your attorney about that. It's a misdemeanor charge that can probably be lifted over time. But again, speak with your lawyer about it," said Detective O'Malley. At that moment our attorney, Asia, entered the room.

"I'll let you guys talk things over. When you're ready, just come into the room next door," Detective O'Malley said as he exited.

I once again explained to Asia and my dad. Once Asia

had heard all of the facts she agreed that the best option was to take the charge of joyriding and then have it removed later.

Jordan was very upset and frustrated with me but said, "I'm glad you're okay. I'm thankful that you weren't shot, wounded or killed. The car isn't worth you losing your life. I can always get another car, but I can't get another you. And I don't care what kind of trouble you're in. You call me. Not your grandmother. Understood?"

"Yeah," I answered. Jordan hugged me and then we all got up to go to the next room to fill out the paper-work.

"What about Keysha?" I asked.

"Your mother is trying to find out about her now," Jordan said.

"She's still being questioned," Asia said. "I'll find out what room they have her in and let you know. The police are just going to have you fill out paperwork releasing Mike into your custody. It's pretty simple."

"Go find out about Keysha. I'll handle things on this end and then join you in a moment," Jordan said as Asia rushed off down the corridor.

nineteen

KEYSHA
Saturday, March 1st

After I was taken to the police station, I was allowed to make a phone call. Since I couldn't reach Jordan earlier I called Barbara. I explained as best I could what had happened and told her where Mike and I were. Without hesitation or biting remarks, Barbara said that she'd have Jordan contact our attorney and that they'd be there right away.

Once I ended my conversation with Barbara, the investigators placed me inside a small interrogation room and began grilling me for about two hours about Mike, Jordan's car and the paper-wrapped money from the Currency Exchange that was found inside my purse. I told them at least one hundred times what had happened but they seemed to have a difficult time believing my story. Then they asked me if I'd be willing to be placed in a police lineup. I agreed to it because I knew that no witnesses would be able to say that I was there. The police had me and about five other girls place a bandana on the lower half of our faces. We looked like we were about to go rob a train or something. After going through the humiliation of being placed in a police lineup, I was marched back to the interrogation room, where I just sat and waited.

Finally a female detective entered the interrogation room. She was a rather tall woman with gingerbread skin, a short Afro, a caring smile and warm eyes. She didn't appear to be the typical hardnosed officer.

"Hello, Keysha," she said as she shut the door behind her.

"Hey," I said, and I sat nervously. My skin was once again itching like wildfire because I was so stressed out. I tried hard not to scratch but I couldn't control myself.

"My name is Officer Davis," she said as she sat down across the table.

"I've already told the other officer that I didn't do it. Why are you guys still holding me?" I asked.

"I'm one of the investigators looking into the Currency Exchange robbery," she explained. "I just want to make sure that I've got a few things straight, okay?"

"There is nothing more to tell. I've told you everything that I know. I want to go home," I said with a shaky voice.

"I know this seems repetitive, Keysha, but can you tell me once again how you got this money?" Officer Davis asked.

"Oh God," I said as I raised the palms of my hands and

buried my face in them. I took a few deep breaths and started crying. When I was done, I pulled myself together and launched into my story. After asking me a series of probing questions, Officer Davis seemed satisfied with my statement.

"Okay." Officer Davis exhaled as she stood up and moved towards the door.

"What now? Please don't send another person in here and make me tell that entire story again," I said.

"Just sit tight. I need to verify your version of what happened," she said and then left the room.

Another hour passed before the door opened up. When I looked up I saw Jordan, Barbara, Mike and Asia enter the room.

"It's about time!" I said with tearful joy. "Can I go now?"

"Yes. You're free to go now," said Asia. I stood up and went over to give Barbara and Jordan big hugs.

"I'm not giving you a hug because you're crazy," I said to Mike.

"I'm so sorry, Keysha. I messed up big time. I'm sorry for everything. These past few weeks I've treated you badly and I had no reason to."

"You're doggone right you've been treating me badly." I wasn't willing to let him off the hook just yet.

"When we get back home we're going to discuss all of this. I'm sure that we'll find the lesson to be learned when we're done," said Barbara, who began rubbing my back in an effort to comfort me.

"Can you forgive me, Keysha?' Mike asked.

"Yeah, but it's going to cost you. No more making fun

of my skin. No more yelling at me about the bathroom. And you have to do my chores for at least two months."

"Agreed," Mike said and then stepped over and hugged me tight. "Thank you for helping me stop myself before things got any worse," he whispered in my ear.

"Okay," I said as I welcomed his embrace. "Now, let me go, you're making me cry." I said.

"I'm glad all of this is over," said Jordan.

"So what happened? Did they finally believe me?" I asked.

"I got them to drop the charges against you," said Asia.

"They were going to actually charge me?" I was blown away when she said that.

"The police caught Simon, who cooperated with police in order to get leniency. Simon said that he and Justine would have gotten away had you not delayed them. He also admitted that you knew nothing of what he and Justine planned to do and confirmed that you tried to talk her out of going with him."

"So where's my Mom at?" I asked.

"The police are still searching for her and your baby brother. Simon says that they got into an argument and went their separate ways. He says that he dropped her off at a bus station. Since your mother is now a fugitive, I'm certain the court will terminate her visitation rights," said Asia. I didn't know how I felt about that. It was sad not knowing when or where I'd see my mother and baby brother again, but then again I was glad that all the drama with Justine was over and done with for now.

"Do you know what's going to happen with Toya?" I asked.

"Who cares," Mike spat. "Don't even mention that girl's name around me."

'She's probably going to be charged with auto theft and sent to juvie until her court hearing," said Asia.

"I hope they throw the book at her," Mike said as we exited the room. We all went into a small room where Jordan filled out some paperwork and all of my belongings, which had been taken when I arrived, were returned to me. When I got my cell phone back I noticed that Wesley had called me several times. I stepped away from my family for a little privacy and called Wesley.

"Hello," the voice of an elderly woman answered Wesley's phone.

"Oh, I'm sorry, I must have the wrong number," I said and was about to hang up.

"Is this Keysha?" the elderly woman asked.

"Yes. Who is this?" I asked.

"This is Wesley's grandmother." She paused for a moment as she coughed. She cleared her throat and said, "Sugar, I'm afraid that I've got some bad news." Her voice was shaky and uncertain.

"Bad news?" I asked, not really certain if I heard her correctly.

'Yes. Wesley has been shot."

* * * * *

DISCUSSION QUESTIONS

1. Why do you think Mike was willing to risk everything to be with Toya?

2. Discuss how and why Toya was able to connect with Mike and manipulate him so well.

3. Mike took Jordan's car without his permission and subsequently had it stolen from him. If you were Mike, how would you have handled a crisis like the one he had to deal with?

4. Sabrina really likes Mike a lot and wants to make him happy. However, Mike is putting pressure on her to have sex with him. Having sex before marriage makes Sabrina uncomfortable and puts a strain on her relationship with Mike. Discuss how you'd handle a situation where someone wanted you to do something you're not comfortable with. Would you break your rules or go against your values to make them happy? Why or why not?

5. Keysha learns that she must return to her old neighborhood and visit with her mother. Do you think the judge should have allowed Justine visitation rights? Why or why not?

6. Discuss Justine's motivation for reentering Keysha's life.

7. If you were Keysha and were faced with the option of returning stolen money or helping Mike deal with his crisis, what would you have done and why?

8. What are the lessons that both Keysha and Mike learned?

9. Do you have any friends or know of someone who has had to deal with the issue of peer pressure and sex?

10. Do you have any friends or know of someone who has suddenly become rebellious or defiant and is heading towards trouble?

11. What was your favorite part of the book? Why?